SCRATCHING
THE SURFACE

*For Carolyn,
my ray of sunshine.*

UNDERTOW

PUBLICATIONS

2013

2013 Trade Edition: ISBN 978-0-9813177-1-7
Copyright © 2013 Undertow Publications
Cover design copyright © 2013 John Oakey
Interior design, typesetting, and layout by Michael Kelly
A Murder of Crows copyright © 2013 Brian A. Hopkins
The Library of Babel—Short by One Volume copyright © 2007 John
Pelan

All stories copyright © Michael Kelly

SECOND EDITION

Undertow Publications
Pickering, ON Canada
undertowbooks@gmail.com

TABLE OF CONTENTS

AUTHOR'S NOTE

In early 2007 my first collection of short stories, *Scratching the Surface*, which you now hold in your hands, was published by a small press in Wales, and debuted at the World Horror Convention in Toronto, Canada. A few weeks after the convention, the press folded. It was an inauspicious debut, to be sure.

Original copies of the collection are listed for hundreds of dollars on various book-selling sites. Not because of its literary merit, but by virtue of being a rarity. I decided it was time to put out another affordable edition of the book, if only to give it a bit of life after its aborted debut.

This edition of the collection mirrors the first, warts and all, except for a couple of exceptions: I have a new cover, and I've added Brian Hopkins' afterword, which was unfairly excised by the publisher in the first edition.

If you enjoy this collection, I hope you will seek out my second collection, Undertow & Other Laments, available from Dark Regions Press in the United States.

Michael Kelly
Pickering, ON
May 2013

THE LIBRARY OF BABEL: SHORT BY ONE VOLUME

Ever since reading Borges' wonderful "Library of Babel" I've been fascinated by the idea of books that either ought to have been written or books that ought to have been published. Fortunately, as a writer and publisher I'm able to at least make a dent in the very long lists... In some cases, the books that ought to have been written are far beyond my power or that of anyone else... I can't think of any way that we'd be able to have things like the revised version of *Titus Alone* written by a hale and hearty Mervyn Peake or *Fifty Years of Henry Kuttner*, (the twenty-volume set), though other dream books like The *Collected Works* of Gary Braunbeck and *100 Stories* by Joel Lane remain in realm of possibility. As a publisher, I occasionally get to make some of these dreams become realities, and in some cases I simply miss the boat... . In the case of the present volume, to use newspaper parlance, I was scooped.

I've been a Michael Kelly fan a long time... . Yes, I've been reading Michael Kelly for more years than would be kind to either of us for me to enumerate. How did this book get away? I don't know... . I can say without rancor or (much) jealousy that Sean Wright of Crowswing Books was just quicker on the draw than I was.

Quite frankly, I wasn't sure that Michael had enough short stories out there to fill a whole book and I say this with the caveat that I assiduously look for his stories on a regular basis with the foreknowledge that as a craftsman of the highest order, he's not terribly prolific and one can keep abreast of his output fairly easily. Somehow the fact that along with the two stories I'd bought for various anthologies and some dozen others that I'd read, Michael had quietly amassed enough tales to fill a volume and I had simply missed the boat.

The great news is that *Scratching the Surface* may now be removed from the library of Babel and read by a wider audience (as it so well deserves). If you've read some of Michael's work before, than you know that you're in for an adventurous read... It may not be entirely pleasant, Kelly has the same eye for the bleak and despairing that you find with the great works of Brian Hodge and Joel Lane. These are stories that not only make you think, they make you *feel*. And they sneak back up on you days or weeks later and make you *feel* again. It's been said that the point of art is to disturb, and if that is the case than what Michael Kelly does is most definitely art. There are dozens of horror writers that can cause horripilations when reading a piece for the first time. There are but a select few that can write fiction that not only has an impact on the first reading, but will sneak up on you days, weeks, or even years later and *pounce*; ripping your comfort zone to shreds. Charles Beaumont had the gift, Dennis Etchison has it, and most definitely Michael Kelly has it.

If you're not the sort of person that appreciates fiction powerful enough to make you look over your shoulder just to check that the street you're walking down hasn't somehow *changed* and that the status quo of the mundane is still intact; then give this book to someone else! On the other hand, if you're the adventurous sort that doesn't mind taking a close look at the human condition through a glass darkly, then I invite you to take a walk on the dark side with Michael Kelly. It may not be an entirely comfortable journey, but it will be a trip well worth taking.

John Pelan
September 2007

SCRATCHING THE SURFACE

My time with Silva was short, but memorable. I remember it, all of it, like it was yesterday. I remember it with a sharp clarity that never existed in his photographs. Though, upon reflection, one could clearly see the real world swirling beneath the surface of his nightmarish portraits. It was an irony not lost on Silva, I'm sure.

He arrived one rainy, windy night in the Spring. It was a damp, miserable May and my twelve-year-old hands were already experiencing throbbing bouts of arthritic pain that plague me to this day.

Where he came from, I still don't know.

I was in the living room reading an Aquaman comic book, sitting close to the radiator for warmth, when I heard a muffled clumping sound from the front porch. It wasn't a knock on the door, just a slight shuffle and stamp, as if an impatient stallion were outside waiting to get in. I put the comic down and cocked an ear, waiting for the sound to return, but it didn't. So I waited and waited for what seemed an interminable amount of time, leaning forward, listening as the clock on the mantle ticked . . . ticked . . ., as the water hissed and steamed through the radiator, then, THUMP-THUMP on the wooden door and I nearly jumped out of my skin.

I stood, my heart beating inexplicably fast. Mum and Dad were in the kitchen, their voices oddly muted. I stepped lightly to the door, bent to press an ear to the old warped wood.

THUMP!

I shrank back, then laughed. What was I afraid of? Mum and Dad were home.

I grasped the brass doorknob, gave it a quick twist and pulled the door open. It was dark and wet outside, the kind of darkness that is somehow thicker, more solid than it ought to be; a deep black darkness that suggests damp mystery. Of course, I was but twelve years of age, and given to fits of imaginative fancy. Perhaps it was just another wet night like any other.

At any rate, I peered into the void. At first, I saw nothing at all but the rain washing by in cool sheets. The porch light was obviously out. Then, slowly, as my eyes adjusted to the gloom, I glimpsed a form take shape. The figure stepped forward, and I took an involuntary step back. It was a man, tall as the day is long. Of his physical features, I could discern nothing. He wore a dingy grey slicker (what Mum would have called a mackintosh), one of those wide fisherman's hats that neatly deflected the rain, and dungarees tucked into black rubber boots.

The strange man—and even before I got to know him, just looking at him then and there, my adolescent mind knew Silva was a strange man—leaned into the doorway, doffed his fisherman's hat and bent regally, sweeping his arm before him, as if presenting himself to royalty.

"Silva," was all he said.

I squinted up at him. The man's coal black hair was stuck to his head in a pointy, barb wire tangle. It didn't look so much wet as it did greasy. One large dark eyebrow cut a line across his forehead. His face was round, almost cherubic, with puffy pale cheeks and, yes, a button nose. The whole effect was oddly incongruent on such a tall person. You come to expect a certain gauntness to tall, thin people. And under his slicker, I could tell that Silva was thin. You expect sunken bony cheeks, deep-set eyes. You don't expect a face that would be more at home on a toddler, the eyebrow notwithstanding.

And his eyes were a rich raven black, strangely iridescent. I couldn't differentiate the pupil from the iris. They shimmered and wavered like an oil slick. I remember feeling faintly sick to my stomach as I gazed at Silva's eyes. A warm wave of dizziness passed through me.

Silva stepped forward, into the house. He stared down at me, a thin dark shadow. Of course, at the time, I didn't know him. He was just a strange wet man standing in our doorway.

I stood, looking up at Silva, trying not to look into those swirling eyes, but unable to look away. His face shone waxy in the wan light, and patches of dry skin peeled off in tiny flakes. My hands were bunching in the front folds of my shirt. I recall this because my fingers were stiff and sore from the damp.

Finally, after what seemed minutes but was likely only seconds, I tried to speak. "D-Dad? D-Dad?"

Then Dad was there, behind me, his hands on my shoulders. "Well, Nate, I see you've met Mister Silva." Dad grinned. "Go on, then, Nate. Introduce yourself proper."

I relaxed my hands, stuck one out. "Pleased to meet you, Mr. Silva."

Silva looked at my hand, gripped it gently, as if he knew it was aching. His palm was moist and damp and cool all at once.

"Likewise, Nathaniel." He rubbed the top of my hand, stared at it curiously. "Your tiny hand is frozen."

"Bad circulation," I said.

"Yes, well, I'm very pleased to make your acquaintance," he said. "I'm Silva."

His voice, like his appearance, was a strange contrast. It was soft rain and a scratchy jangle. And he'd called me Nathaniel. No one ever called me Nathaniel. To Dad I was Nate. To Mum, Nathan.

And he was Silva. Just Silva.

Dad had stepped around and was shaking Silva's hand. "Welcome Mr. Silva. With the weather like it is, wasn't sure if you'd be delayed."

"Bus was right on time," Silva said.

Mum was behind me, hovering, keeping well back. Silva looked past me, in Mum's direction.

"Good evening, Mrs. Swann," Silva said.

Mum nodded, almost imperceptibly.

"Nate," Dad said, "Mr. Silva has let the room."

Our house, like many in the neighborhood, had a room at the side accessible from doors inside and outside the house. Just a room with a bed, a desk, a small closet, a tiny ice chest and a small bathroom. Dad had been trying to rent the room for some time now. There had been a baby boom, sure, but the economic boom hadn't come to fruition. We weren't in a bad way, Dad could still buy me the occasional comic book and soda (his idea of love), but the extra money would surely come in handy. At least Dad thought so.

So now, we had a stranger in the house.

Mum, I could see, was none too pleased.

ᎶᎧᏠ

After that first night, Silva quickly settled in. Mum was distrustful of him at first, peering at him surreptitiously whenever they crossed paths. But she soon relaxed, paying him no heed. Dad was happy and exuberant to have him around, chatting amiably on the rare occasions he saw Silva.

And me? Well, I was pleased to have someone else around, frankly. I was a bit of a loner, with no real friends, and no prospects of ever being part of the mainstream crowd. My parents paid me about as much attention as they did a house plant; a little water, a little sun, the occasional kind word. Here, in Silva, was another person, a man no less, alone with no friends or family to speak of.

Yet the fact was, Silva was somewhat reclusive. Which, to an inquisitive twelve year old, was tantamount to an invitation to pry. And he had people, mostly local people of passing acquaintance, and some strangers, coming to his side door at odd hours. Perhaps, I thought, he wasn't so lonely as me. Maybe he had many friends. But I dismissed that. Silva didn't seem the type. He was just too . . . odd. Whenever people would come by his place, I would tip-toe over to his door on the inside of our house and gently press a glass to the wood, my ear fixed to the base, and listen for any tell-tale sign of. . . well, anything my twelve year old mind could fathom. And it could fathom a lot. Each time I did this, and I have to admit it was quite often, odd lilting sounds and toneless conversations would filter back to me, as if I were underwater.

So, upon constantly hearing strange noises from the rented room—muted whirrs and thumps and the sound of liquid sloshing—I naturally had to snoop.

One weekend morning, with Mum and Dad downtown, I sat in our kitchen, waiting, knowing Silva's Saturday schedule. Soon enough I witnessed Silva swoosh by the window like a black wraith, his dark coat flapping bat-like. His pale, blurry, round face turned my way, fixed me with a strange grin, then he was gone, down the sidewalk and out of sight.

I stood, crept to the inside door and tried the handle. It was locked, as I knew it would be, so I went out our front door and around the side to Silva's exterior door. This door, to my surprise, was unlocked. Letting myself in, I stood in the small room and let my eyes adjust to the gloom. A faintly unpleasant scent of ammonia filled the dank room.

Silva had tacked up a large burlap canvas sheet, essentially cutting the room in two. His bed was shoved into a far dark corner, seemingly forgotten. A camera (A Hasselblad I would later learn) sat on a tripod near the bed. The wall behind his bed was covered in black and white photographs, tacked at curiously odd angles. The photos fluttered, waved in some illusive breeze.

A chill ran through me, sparking gooseflesh, but I didn't leave, *couldn't* leave. I felt compelled to stay, even though some distant part of my young mind knew that what I was doing was wrong. My hands throbbed in pain. Turning, I studied the canvas wall, which also seemed to shimmer of its own accord. I noticed a small breach at one end of the canvas and slipped through it. I gasped. Sallow amber light flooded the makeshift room like some nightmare Dali vista. That strange scent of ammonia was almost overpowering. A long table had been set up, holding shiny metal canisters and trays of liquid from which emanated that smell. Alongside the trays was what looked like an inverted camera on two rails that ran from the tabletop.

Silva, it seemed, was a photographer. This was his darkroom.

I poked around a bit then carefully backed out of the darkroom and promptly bumped into Silva, who was standing expectantly, hands on hips, staring down at me.

I looked into Silva's face and felt a peculiar calm wash over me. His face seemed to pulse, and the dry flaky patches that interspersed the waxy areas peeled and fell off, drifting like snowflakes to the bare floorboards. My fingers bent and twisted in the folds of my shirt. I had a sudden urge to reach up and touch

Silva's queer face. I had the feeling that it throbbed with the same pain that coursed through my hands.

"Hello, Nathaniel Swann."

"Hello," I answered, unafraid.

"Do you like it?"

"What?"

"My studio," Silva said.

I glanced around. Yes, of course, the canvas acted as both a darkroom and a backdrop for Silva's photographs. It was quite clever.

"Yes," I said.

"Good. And your curiosity has been satiated?"

"Um, yes, I, you see the door was not locked."

Silva fixed me with his black shiny eyes. His one long eyebrow furrowed. "But it was closed," he said.

I had no answer for that, so I just nodded weakly.

Silva smiled. "No harm. You're a boy, and boys as a rule are curious. It's good to have an inquisitive nature, Nathaniel. Don't you agree?"

"Yes, sir."

"Silva, Mr. Swann." He grinned. "Call me Silva."

"You're a photographer?" I asked.

"No more. I'm getting out of the business."

"Why?"

Silva chuckled, but there was no mirth in it. His face twitched and he winced. "I'm tired, Nathaniel. That's all. It's time."

I rubbed my hands, tried to get the blood circulating in them. "But what will you do?"

This time Silva smiled. "So many questions. Nothing. I'll do nothing.

Silva turned abruptly, strode over to the wall tacked with photographs. "My art," he said winsomely, and it seemed he was talking to himself.

I took that as an invitation and went over to stand beside the tall man. I gazed up at him. His face pulsed red. His hands reached up for his face, stopped at his shoulders and reached out to the wall. His fingertips brushed the photographs lightly, reverentially.

14

Turning, I studied the photographs. They were portraits of people, individuals and families, but like no portraits I'd ever seen. I stepped closer, squinted up at the pictures. All the images were distorted, the corners of the photos seemingly pulling taut, the middles round, bulbous, beating like a heart. Of course it couldn't be real, I told myself then. It's just trick photography, a certain treatment of light and shadow, black and white, a dozen different shades of grey.

But that wasn't the worst part, no. The faces on the subjects were all slightly misshapen, their eyes stretched sideways, their noses askew, and their mouths a long oblong rictus. I blanched, tottered backward.

Silva caught me by the elbow. "It's okay, Nathaniel. Don't be afraid. It's my gift."

My hands burned with pain. I wanted to scream but couldn't. My mouth worked wordlessly like a fish out of water. My stomach fluttered and I spun, ran out the door and back to my house, to our bathroom, where I slumped beside the toilet and retched into the porcelain bowl.

CB80

The next day, Sunday, I returned to Silva's room. He answered the door before I even finished knocking, as if he were waiting for me. I believe he was. His face twitched, spasmed. His eyes were like shiny black stones on the bottom of a cool riverbed.

Silva stood aside. "Come in, Nathaniel."

I stepped into the small room, walked gingerly to the wavering wall of photographs.

"How?" I asked, though I didn't really know what I was asking.

Silva sighed, though he didn't sound close by. "My art. My gift, my curse. I don't know."

"Wh-Who would buy these. . . pictures?"

Silva's voice floated on the air. "Oh, no one would want these, Nathaniel. I give them what they want. I give them what they pay for. And I take what I need."

A silence ensued as I studied the malformed and distorted faces that leered grotesquely from the wall.

Then, "Come, Nathaniel, I'll show you."

Silva disappeared behind the canvas. I followed him into the makeshift room. The amber-colored safe light hanging in one corner gave the room an otherworldly glow.

Silva opened a drawer under the table, pulled out sheets of negatives. He fed a single strip of negative into a holder, then inserted it into the enlarger, between the bellows and the body. Silva flipped a switch and the enlarger hummed to life, projecting a blurry image onto an easel on the table. He reached up, turned a knob and the image came into sharp focus. Then Silva switched the enlarger off.

"Are you watching, Nathaniel?" Silva turned, stared at me, his face flowing, dripping like warm putty in the wan sallow light of the darkroom. "Some day this may be you. You will be the creator, the artist."

I smiled weakly, brought my hands up, studied them. "Not with these hands."

Silva slipped a sheet of paper from a black box and slid it into the easel. He turned on the enlarger, tapped the tabletop ten times, then turned it off. He pulled the paper from the easel, slid it into the first tray and proceeded to lift and tilt the tray, letting the liquid cover the surface of the paper.

"Developer," Silva said.

I stepped closer, peered into the tray. Slowly, an image took shape, a portrait of a man. After a while, when the image had fully formed, Silva lifted the sheet of paper from the tray with wooden tongs and deposited into the next liquid-filled tray.

"Fixer," Silva intoned.

A few minutes later Silva was putting the photo into the final tray.

"A stop-bath and a wash," Silva told me.

Done, Silva pulled the wet photo from the tray and dried it with a simple hair dryer lying on the table. He handed the portrait to me. His face, I saw, had stopped fluttering.

"Well, Nathaniel, what do you think?"

I gazed at the picture. It was unremarkable. Even in the half-

16

light I could see it was a simple, smiling portrait of a simple man. No curious eddies or swirls flecked the picture.

I shrugged.

Silva laughed, his voice a harsh bark, a cool wind. He snatched the photo from my hands and quickly ripped it in two, letting the halves fall to the floor.

"A simple man, Nathaniel. A dullard, wasting his life. So why not take some of it? Why not use it if he isn't? It's wasted on him."

Silva leaned in close. His face was flush and heat radiated from it. He smelled of acidic photographic chemicals and I feared a caustic reaction should I accidentally touch him. And I feared something else.

He smiled strangely. "Everyone's afraid to die, Nathaniel. Even me. Especially me." Silva paused. His voice grew faint. "At least I was at one time. Now I'm just weary." He shook his head, continued. "It's okay to be afraid. At least you have feelings. At least you're alive. I don't trouble those people." Silva straightened. His face drooped and he stared past me, blankly, as if I wasn't there. I didn't care for the tone of his last sentence. Didn't care for the way he said trouble.

"But some, Nathaniel, are afraid to *live*. They wake each day in drudgery, trudging off to work, blindly performing their menial tasks by rote. Then they return, to sit and stare at the television as their dinners congeal in their laps, no words issuing from their closed mouths." Silva trembled. "They are blind, Nathaniel, their staring eyes flitting over the wondrous minutiae of everyday life, just barely scratching the surface."

I thought of my parents.

"Don't be afraid to live your life, Nathaniel."

Silva shook his head, grinned, stared down at me with his oil slick eyes. "Those people are just taking up space. They are already dead."

I gulped.

Silva turned back to the table. "Okay, Nathaniel, watch. *Really* watch."

Again he grabbed a sheet of paper from the box and stuck it in the easel. Before he turned on the enlarger he placed his fingers on the smooth sheet.

"This is my art, Nathaniel."

Silva smoothed and polished the paper with his fingertips. His hands moved with a liquid grace. He prodded and probed the picture.

"You have to work the skin, the emulsion, make it malleable."

He switched on the enlarger, tapped off ten seconds, then placed the paper into the first tray. The image began to form. Silva dipped his fingers in the tray, worked them over the photograph like a baker kneading bread. He removed the soaking sheet of paper, dropped it into the next tray. Again he worked the image with his bare hands, employing his knuckles and nails, his palms and the heel of his hands, rolling them over and pushing then through the sticky emulsion. Silva dropped the photograph into the final tray, letting it rest several minutes, then pulled it out and placed the sopping image onto the tabletop.

Silva bent over the portrait. The air in the room wavered. Once again the sickly glow made Silva's head appear to shimmer and pulse. His frenzied fingers danced and skipped atop the wet photo, rubbing, smoothing, polishing the emulsion. He was scratching the surface, peeling away tiny flecks of what looked like skin.

Quickly, Silva dried the print and scurried out of the room. I followed. He stood at his wall, looking at his work, clutching his new piece of art. As I approached he turned to me. His face was crimson and bloated. Heat radiated from it in sickening waves. I reached up and Silva flinched, drew back.

"So very tired, Nathaniel." His cheeks vibrated. "There's no pleasure, no peace in the work anymore."

He handed me the photograph. "This is the real portrait," Silva said. "The deceit unmasked."

I stared at it. It was no longer a simple portrait of a simple man. The photo appeared to glow with its own light. The black shadows slithered, the highlights sparkled, gradating shades of grey quivered. The man's eyes bulged bug-eyed, his nose was splayed to ribbons. The mouth stretched sideways, lips cracked, revealing tiny pointy teeth. Something moved deep in the man's maw.

Silva's hot hand on my shoulder made me start. I dropped the photograph.

"It's all a facade, Nathaniel. The faces aren't real. It's just a skin, hiding what's underneath. And underneath we are all mostly the same; blood and bone and gristle."

Silva leaned in. His face was pulsating and peeling. "Can you see the real me?"

I took my leave then, scared of what I would do. Scared of what might happen.

It was the last time I saw Silva alive.

ᗋᔐᗌ

All the next week I busied myself with school and chores, trying to put Silva out of my mind. There came no noises from his room. No visitors came to his door. Curious, I thought. But he did say he was retiring.

My parents continued living their sedate lives, wearing their comfortable masks.

Come Saturday I sat in the kitchen and waited for Silva to go bustling by the window. He didn't, and a queer dread flooded me.

With mounting trepidation I stood and went out to Silva's door. I knocked, but got no answer. Turning the doorknob, I pushed the door inward and stepped into his gloomy room.

Silva was prone, face up, in the middle of his tiny room. I stumbled over to him. Gazing down at Silva I wept. Great sobs racked my body. It was the first time I'd ever cried and it felt good. It was real. I was *alive*.

Composing myself, I knelt beside Silva, gazed down at his grim countenance. His eyes shone blackly. His lips were pulled back in a smile or a grimace. On his chest, gripped in one clawed hand, was a photograph. I plucked the photo from his fingers, brought it up to eye level. It was a picture of himself, of Silva. His face was calm, his skin clear, unmarked, almost luminous. A remarkable portrait.

I turned the photo over. Written on the back was *Can you see the real me?*

I tucked the photograph into my waistband.

My fingers clenched. My hands screamed in agony, throbbed

19

with deep pain. I knew what I had to do.

I bent, placed my fingers on his waxy face. I brushed my fingertips along his patchwork skin, skimming the surface. My fingers swirled, danced, probed. I rubbed, lightly at first, then harder, digging my nails into the spongy, dead skin and peeled back, bit by bit, long strips of parchment-like skin. I scratched, pulled, peeled. I dug at the flesh with nubby bloody fingers, raking them across his face repeatedly until I hit muscle and tissue, sinew and bone. Scratching until I saw Silva, the real Silva, all blood and bone gristle, behind the facade.

Smiling, I went home to wash my hands.

CRSO

I still have all of Silva's equipment. As I suspected, there was no family, no persons who came forward to make any claim to what little Silva possessed. It was given to my parents, who originally had wanted to sell it off to make a quick buck. But after some gentle pleading, convincing them I'd never want for anything else, I eventually coerced them into letting me have it. His camera, the trays, the canvas sheet, the enlarger, all sit in a dusty closet in my modest apartment.

And I still have his self-portrait. It is tacked to the wall where I can see it. Lately it has begun to fade and crack, the emulsion flaking and peeling.

I've begun to think that I might take up photography. My hands still pain me, giving me pause to those thoughts, but something else compels me.

You see, it's my face. I study it in the mirror. If I look close enough I can see tiny ripples, little pockets of flesh that pulse and move beneath the surface. And it hurts. How it hurts. It burns with an intense fever-heat. I want to reach up, rip the skin from the bone, rid myself of this false mask. But I don't. The pain reminds me that I'm alive.

So, I stay my hand. I sit and stare at the closet, my face and hands in agony. Perhaps, like my friend Silva, if I dig below the surface I can seek some succor in the lives of ordinary men.

THIN RED WIRE

The Kickers are out. He hears them, howling like monkeys. They'd caught someone or something.

Harn strides down the crooked sidewalk, toward the delighted screeching, past row after row of sad brown houses with crumbling bricks, boarded windows, and weed-choked lawns. A home like his own. Many of the houses have signs out front, in crude black paint. KEEP OUT! proclaims a sign. Another reads: TRESPASSERS WILL BE SHOT! He passes by a squat bungalow with a sagging porch. A fat, shirtless man stares at him warily from the shadows. No one else is about, though he can sense people watching, peering through dirty, broken windows to the dirty, broken street pocked with holes. Even if buses and taxi-cabs traveled to this part of the city, they'd never survive the pitted roads.

Smoke from nearby fires stings his nostrils. A grey haze floats in the air. Through the foggy miasma he sees the sun, a dull flat nickel. The wind blows hot and suffocating. He pictures the homeless on Shuter street huddled around large metal cans, burning scraps of stolen wood, flames licking the air, each person rubbing their hands in front of their own private inferno. And he pictures the homeless, when they get wind of the Kickers, scattering like cockroaches in a bright light. He hardly blames them.

Under the acrid tang of the smoke, he smells dead fish. The river, he recalls, is as dead as the city. Oily and stagnant, covered in green scum. A dumping ground.

Harn stops at the end of the street, glances up. As always, the pale face stares impassively, unblinking, unsmiling, expectant, gazing up to the heavens. Moon-Pie. He likes it. The kid has a moon-pie face. Round and white and open. The boy is 11 or 12 years old. Fuck, who knows, maybe he's 14. Children, like many things, are a mystery to him.

The boy stares from the third-floor window of a crumbling Victorian brownstone. A pallid, unsmiling face floating behind a grease-smeared window. Always watching. Harn wishes the boy would leave the window. Wishes he would go inside and play a vid. Someone will notice the boy one day and take an interest. The boy's eyes flick to Harn, regard him with mild curiosity.

Harn sighs, turns the corner, and sees the Kickers. There are three of them; wire-thin, blue jeans, black leather jacket, white T's, and black Doc Martens gleaming in the twilight. A living, breathing cliché from some ancient pre-digital vid. There is no spark of originality in the Kickers. Like everything these days, it is easier to appropriate from the past. Harn can see the fever glint in their eyes as the black boots kick and kick and kick. There's a brown and bloody mess on the ground beneath their feet. Their cackles pierce the hot, thick air.

Harn walks toward the Kickers, stops a few feet away. They look up.

"What's this, then?" asks one, looking Harn up and down, taking an involuntary step back. "You wired?"

As if on cue, the wire pulses faintly.

The Kickers can tell. Like them, he is different. Though he has no choice in the matter.

One of the Kickers gives a last quick kick to the pulpy mess, then they turn and run shrieking down the narrow street like a gaggle of schoolchildren. The Kickers stay well clear of Harn. He's treated like a contagion. And that's perfectly fine with him.

He walks over to the brown mess, leans down. A dog. Or what's left of it. The head is cracked and leaking, the ribs kicked in. Harn wonders about the terror it felt.

A sound reaches Harn. A short, sharp yelp. Across the street a cardboard box skitters along the pavement. He crosses the cracked asphalt, scoops up the box, and uncovers a tiny black dog. A puppy. The puppy crouches, trembles, barks at Harn. He bends, picks up the tiny ball of fury, and places it in his jacket pocket.

Harn turns and walks away. Sometimes, he thinks he's living in a dream.

ॐ

The dream went like this:

A woman in white was talking. Her voice was silk and smoke. "You'll become drowsy, you'll drift, and then you'll sleep. You may dream, but you will not be aware of your surroundings."

The woman touched Harn's arm. "Won't feel a thing."

Harn squirmed. He'd felt her touch, hadn't he?

"It's a very quick procedure," the woman continued. She leaned over Harn and smiled. "Easy-peasey, pudding and pie. You'll awake a better man."

Harn's heart raced. He tried to turn his head, lift an arm, but the straps held him tight. He breathed deep.

"That's right," said the woman in white, "try and relax."

He tried to speak. His mouth wouldn't move.

The woman stroked his cheek. Harn shivered. The woman laughed. "There's nothing to be afraid of."

The pungent stench of antiseptic stung his nostrils. The woman (doctor?) turned and fiddled with tiny silver devices on a tray beside him. "The Amygdala is a portion of the brain located in the medial temporal lobe," she said. She leaned over, gave him a wry smile. "I don't expect you to understand any of this, but it helps me to talk it out.

"It is the size and shape of an almond. That's how it got its name. Amygdala is Greek for almond. It is a set of subcortical nuclei, part of the limbic system." She grinned. A parent schooling a child. "Fascinating, no?"

Harn blinked.

The woman in white turned back to her tray of metal instruments, rearranged them. "There are lots of important nerves coursing along the Amygdala," she continued. "They connect to your neocortex, for instance." She tapped Harn's head with a finger, and he flinched.

"My, my," she said. "Why so jumpy?

23

"All those tiny circuits regulate your emotions, your feelings. We've isolated the crucial circuit – let's call it the "fear factor" – that controls your fears and phobias, your anger and anxiety." Her grin widened. "And we'll cut it out." She paused, rubbed at a tiny dark spot on her white smock. "The case studies prove this works. By ridding the brain of the fear factor, you can't feel fear. Your anger will be suppressed. So," she rubbed her hands, "you'll be much less likely to revert to your previous ways. A small price to pay, don't you think?"

Harn closed his eyes, drifted. A corona of bright stars winked across his vision.

"Of course," the woman continued, "when we first started the procedures there were setbacks. We thought excising those nerves would be enough. It wasn't. Circuits don't work that way. They can't be cut. We found that out the hard way." She sighed. "So we came up with this." She held a tiny half inch piece of red wire between metal tweezers. "A ground wire. That's all it is. We couldn't do the procedure without it. It closes the circuit, so that there won't be any unfortunate mishaps. A thin red wire."

Harn heard the admiration in her voice. Then he heard a metallic whirring buzz, like a dentist's drill. Heat covered his head, as if a brilliant spotlight was turned on.

The woman continued to speak. Her voice sounded far away. "Some *patients* tell us they can feel the wire, sense it. That's impossible. They can't feel a thing. Likely they are experiencing some sort of associative disorder. They know they are wired, so they *think* they can feel it."

Harn floated. He was on a boat, gliding down a river, gazing up at a blanket of brilliant stars. Something buzzed by his ear, like a bee.

From far, far away, he heard her. "Okay, let's get to work."

The bee stung him.

 C380

When Harn awoke, he was staggered by beauty. He saw a black sky dotted with a million winking, glittering lights. Pulsing. A velvet curtain studded with diamonds. An inferno of stars. He gasped.

There came a dull throb, a faint pulse, inside his head. Like an awakening heart. He opened his eyes, blinked. The stars disappeared. He was in a green room with sallow, waxen light. A woman in white smiled at him. His first thought was that she was an angel, then he saw the clipboard, the plastic gloves, and the stethoscope.

"How do you feel?" the woman asked.

Harn was silent. He blinked, stared at the green walls.

"Good as new," the woman said, answering for Harn. "Better, in fact."

And then Harn felt it again, a faint pulsing in his head. The wire.

It all seemed like a dream.

And he wasn't afraid.

಄಄

"You're late." Fathead wipes greasy hands on a greasy, blood-stained apron. Fathead's real name is Teddy. Harn prefers Fathead.

Harn takes off his jacket, hangs it on the hook by the door. The puppy's black head peeks from the pocket. The puppy yelps.

"No pets." Fathead's face is the colour of wet cement.

"I found him," Harn says.

Fathead unwraps his soiled apron, shoves it into Harn's chest. "Keep the thing quiet. I don't want it bothering the customers."

Harn nods. "Sure."

Fathead goes to the back door, stops and looks back at Harn. "Don't be late again."

"Sure, Fa—Sure, boss."

Fathead waddles through the back door and a hot, smoke-tinged wind blows in. Hell's kitchen, Harn thinks.

Harn takes the puppy from the coat and places it on a nearby counter. The puppy licks his hand. Harn ties the apron around his waist and goes over to the refrigerator. He pulls a tray of burgers

25

from a rack and hands one to the puppy. The small dog gulps it down. Done, the puppy yelps, wags its tail. Harn fetches a bowl of water for the dog.

The door from the dining area swings open and Judy Blue-Eyes walks in, whistling. "Hey, Sugar," she says. "How ya doing?" Harn smiles. "Good."

Judy Blue-Eyes points to the dog. "Who's your friend?"

"Puppy," Harn answers. "I found him."

"Cute little fellow." Judy winks. "Like you."

Harn looks down. His face flushes.

"You ain't much for words, are you, kid?" Judy says.

"Guess not," Harn says. "Words can get you in trouble."

Judy grins, clips two chits above the grill. "Need a burger platter and liver and onions."

Harn leans over the grill and gets to work. Puppy sleeps on the counter. Judy Blue-Eyes is in and out of the kitchen, placing orders, taking plates of food out to the customers. Between orders, Harn takes a deep plastic tray out into the dining room to collect dirty dishes. The diner is almost empty now, but two men sit at the counter, a red stool between them like a barrier, talking loudly. One man sips coffee. The other waves a fork.

"There's talk they might wire everyone. They can do the procedure on babies now, you know. It's in the news vids. Completely up to the parents."

"Procedure? You make it sound like it's no big deal."

"It isn't. Just a little snip."

"Fuck that. The bastards aren't cutting into me."

"What's the problem? It doesn't harm anyone. And we wouldn't have to live like mice anymore, always afraid."

"Better that than to be half a man."

"Think of it—no crime. None."

"At what price?"

"Nothing. There's nothing to lose, and so much to gain."

"Utopia?"

"Maybe. The statistics bear that out."

"Fucking idealist. Who's going to wire the wirers?"

"I don't care for your tone. You can volunteer, you know. Right now. It's a thin red wire. A small operation. Nothing more."

"Please, *friend*, I've seen them. Shuffling about all glassy-eyed." A sip of coffee. "Why don't you bugger off?"

The fork jabs air. "Suit yourself." The man stands, gently places the fork on the chipped countertop, turns to leave. "It's not the end of the world, you know."

Harn steps between the men, scoops the used cutlery and coffee mugs into the tray.

The seated man looks to the departing man, then to Harn. "Isn't it?"

Harn isn't sure if he's being addressed. The thin red wire in his head pulses. He trembles. The tray shakes. He looks at the seated man and shrugs his shoulders. "Beats me."

Judy Blue-Eyes walks by, slaps Harn on the ass. "Go on, Sugar, get back to the grill. Got a mess of orders for you. You'll be swimming in grease."

Harn glances around the dining room. It's empty save for a couple people. He shrugs, marches back to the kitchen, dumps the dirty dishes. Judy Blue-Eyes comes in a moment later.

"You okay, Sugar?"

Harn notices the concern in her voice and in her face. "Yeah, fine. Thanks."

"You looked a little pale back there," Judy Blue-Eyes says. She walks over, leans close to Harn. "You can talk to me, you know. I won't bite."

Harn tries a smile. "I know. Thanks again. It's nothing, really." He looks at Puppy, sitting expectantly on the counter. "I've got a dog now. And he *does* bite."

Judy Blue-Eyes sighs. "A man and his dog. I can bite too," she says, smiling. "If you want."

Harn shuffles his feet. He wonders why he has no interest in Judy Blue-Eyes. She is attractive, kind, and gentle. He could lose himself in her blue-blue tropical ocean eyes.

She takes a step back. "Is there someone else?"

Harn thinks. There isn't anyone else. There's no one. No one but him and Puppy. He wonders if there ever was anyone in his life. He

27

must have had a family. He had parents, didn't he? Everyone has parents. He tries not to think of his parents. Tries not to paint a picture of a past life.

"I'm not ready," Harn says.

"You don't have to be afraid."

Harn remembers waking to an inferno of pulsing stars. "I am not afraid."

Judy Blue-Eyes stares at him, dry-eyed and unblinking. Her eyes are stars. "Could have fooled me," she says.

"You're beautiful," Harn whispers, turning away. And, "I'm sorry."

Judy Blue-Eyes whirls and tramps into the dining room. Puppy yelps and Harn fishes another raw burger out of the refrigerator. Puppy gobbles it down.

෬෫ඐ

It's late and pitch-dark. The streets are empty. No Kickers, no homeless. The wind is still hot, searing a path down narrow back alleys. Tin cans clatter in dry gutters. The air smells of grease and ash. The sky is a great grey cloth covered in smoke and clouds, punched through with black holes. Harn moves along the heaving sidewalk, carrying a sleeping Puppy in his folded arms.

He rounds a corner, heads down the street and stops. Moon-Pie! The boy sits on the concrete steps of the brownstone. He's staring up at the sky.

Harn steps forward. "Hey," he says.

The child looks at him, and Harn is surprised to discover that it is a girl—round, soft, pale face, short-cropped dark hair.

"Hey," the girl mumbles.

"You shouldn't be outside," Harn says. "Not at this hour."

The girl stares at him curiously. "Why not? There's usually no one else out."

Harn has no answer to that.

"Besides," the girl continues, "you're the only one I ever see."

"What are you looking for?" Harn asks. He points. "Up there. You're always looking up there."

28

"The stars. I'd like to see the stars," the girl answers. "The Milky Way. Orion. You know, that sort of thing."

Harn does not know that sort of thing.

"But it's always grey," the girl says

Harn stares skyward. "Yes."

The girl asks, "Have you ever seen the stars?"

Harn trembles, remembering. "Yes."

"What's your name?" the girl asks.

"H-Harn."

The girl crinkles her nose. "Like 'harm'." Even in the near dark Harn sees freckles dotting the girl's face.

"I'm Eadie," she says.

Moon-Pie, Harn thinks. Eadie Moon-Pie.

"Eadie," Harn says. "You should go back inside."

"I can take care of myself."

Harn takes a step closer. Puppy wakes, yelps, wags his tail. "Shush, now, Puppy," Harn says.

Eadie Moon-pie stands, pats Puppy's head. "Cute dog," she says. "I wish I could have a dog."

"It's not safe, Eadie," Harn says. "Aren't you afraid, out here in the dark?"

Eadie Moon-Pie's face is stoic. "The only thing we have to fear is fear itself."

Harn stares at the girl. Puppy leans out, licks her pale, freckled face.

Eadie Moon-Pie laughs. It is sweet summer music. "Nietzsche," she says. "A philosopher." She shrugs, anticipating his question. "I like to read."

"Your parents will be worried," Harn says.

She snorts, glances back at the brownstone. "Hardly," she says. "Besides, you're always out, walking the streets at strange hours. You're not afraid."

It's true. He isn't afraid. But, he realizes, he is concerned *for* Eadie Moon-Pie. And for Puppy. He hugs Puppy close. Is he afraid for them? Is that possible? He wonders if the wire is working.

"No," Harn whispers.

"You're wired," Eadie Moon-Pie says.

Harn blanches. He sits on the cement stairs, puts Puppy down. "Yes" he says.

Eadie Moon-Pie smiles, not unkindly. She shrugs her shoulders. "No big deal."

Harn stares at her. *No big deal*. His head, the thin red wire, pulses. *Thump... thump.* "Thanks," he says.

"Who knows?" Eadie Moon-Pie asks.

Harn stares at her. "My boss. At the diner. It was a condition of employment."

"What about your family?"

Harn looks away, stares at the cement, pets Puppy idly. "I-I don't remember."

Eadie Moon-Pie inches close to him. She smells like a field of lavender blowing in a warm summer wind.

"Do you have family?" she asks.

He looks at her, not a foot away. Her eyes are wide and the colour of the night; a swirling, smoky pool. Puppy lies on a cement stair. "I don't know," he answers. Then, "How old are you?"

"Old enough," she says.

Harn stares, waiting.

"Sixteen," Eadie Moon-Pie says. "Well, tomorrow, really. It's my birthday tomorrow."

"Happy birthday."

She smiles, and Harn smiles watching her smile. "Thanks," she says. "When is your birthday? How old are you?"

Harn lies. "Tomorrow." He lies and smiles. "Twenty-Four."

Eadie Moon-Pie chuckles. "You look older than that."

Harn laughs, short and sad, and picks up Puppy. "Good night, Eadie."

Eadie Moon-Pie's smile fades. "Good night... whoever you are."

"Harn," he says. He holds Puppy up. "And Puppy."

"Good night, Harn." Eadie Moon-Pie stands, rubs Puppy's head. "Night, Puppy."

Harn watches Eadie Moon-Pie skip up the cement stairs. He turns and walks down the dark street. Faintly, on the hot wind, he hears her.

"Happy birthday to us."

Fathead waits for Harn in the kitchen. His round face is flushed and sweating. His brow is furrowed.

Harn nods. "I'm not late, am I?"

Fathead grunts, tosses a dirty rag into a trash can. "No, but you have some explaining to do."

"Oh," Harn says. He pulls Puppy from his jacket, places him on the counter.

"Christ, not that damn dog again," Fathead says. "Leave him home next time."

"Sure," Harn says.

Fathead trundles up to Harn. He smells of grease and dead animals. "What'd you do to Judy?"

Harn blinks, shakes his head. "What do you mean?"

"She's a nice girl," Fathead says. "Don't give her the runaround. Why don't you give her a chance?"

He pictures Eadie Moon-Pie, blurts, "I-I'm seeing someone." The wires pulses. Harn blushes.

Fathead makes fists with his thick meat sausage hands. "Tell her, then. Don't feed her bullshit."

"Sure," Harn says.

"Real talker, aren't you?" Fathead says. "Gotta wonder what she sees in you, kid." He leans close, looks up at Harn. "If she only knew what you done, eh?" Fathead taps the side of Harn's head with a sausage-link finger. "To get that wire. You know? She'd be singing a different tune, my friend."

Harn stumbles back. "W-What did I do?"

Fathead grunts, takes off his apron, balls it between beefy hands and gives it to Harn. "Can't tell ya. Part of the deal. Best you don't know. Best not to think of those things." He brushes past Harn, and through the back door. The wind from Hell blows in.

Harn turns as Judy Blue-Eyes enters the back kitchen. Her hair hangs limply, tangled, and her eyes are deep red and black sockets. She grimaces at Harn.

"Hi," Harn says. The wire beats in his head like a heart.

No response.

She clips an order above the grill. "Toasted western. No ham." Her voice is weary.

Harn wraps the apron around his waist, sidles over to the grill. Judy Blue-Eyes pours coffee.

"Hey," Harn says.

She turns, stares at him. Her blue eyes, deep in her red-rimmed sockets, are clouded over. "Yeah," she says. "What is it?"

Harn looks down, then back up. His hands twist in the folds of the apron. "I wanted to apologize for yesterday. I didn't mean to upset you."

Judy Blue-Eyes shrugs. "Don't worry about it. But can I ask you a question?"

"Sure," Harn says.

"Do you like me?"

"No."

Judy Blue-Eyes blinks, takes a sip of coffee, places the porcelain mug on a table.

Harn disentangles his hands, rubs them on the stained apron. "Yes, I should say. I do like you. Not in *that* way. We can be friends, I hope."

"I see," Judy Blue-Eyes says, her mouth thin and rigid. "Friends. Got plenty of friends. And I've got a brother. I don't need another one."

"I'm sorry," Harn says.

Puppy yelps.

Judy Blue-Eyes squints at Puppy. "Guess a dog is better company than me."

Harn sighs. "It's not you, or Puppy, or Eadie."

"Eadie," Judy Blue-Eyes says. There's resignation in her voice.

Harn says, "It's me." He wants to tell her. He needs to tell her. Needs to tell someone. "I'm wired."

Judy Blue-Eyes mouth gapes. She takes a step back. Her cobalt-blue eyes flash briefly, like dying stars. "Wired," she says. "You've got a goddamn wire."

Harn nods. Puppy sits up on the countertop, barking, tail wagging.

32

Judy Blue-Eyes smiles briefly, but it is an ugly smile, hard and rigid. "To think I almost wasted my time." She laughs, and it is as hard and ugly as her smile. "What did you do? Burn down your house? Hack your father to death?" Judy Blue-Eyes shakes, takes a step forward. Her voice is low, filled with venom. "Or did you rape and strangle some little girl? Or was it a little boy?"

Harn unties the apron, lets it drop to the floor. He turns, scoops up Puppy, goes to the door. There are tears in his eyes, and it takes him aback. He can't ever remember crying.

"That's right," Judy Blue-Eyes says, "get out of here."

Harn pushes the door open. Hot wind sears his face, drying his eyes. The wire beats faintly. *Thump... thump*. He blinks, looks back at Judy Blue-Eyes. She clutches the porcelain mug. Crying, shaking. Judy Blue-Eyes raises the mug, hurls it at him. "Leave, you son-of-a-bitch!" she says. The mug spins through the air, smashes into the side of his head. Stars explode. There's pressure in his head, a punch, a prod, a dim pulse. When he opens his eyes, Judy Blue-Eyes is gone.

Harn, Puppy in pocket, walks out the back door.

CRSO

Eadie Moon-Pie waits for him on the cement stairs. She stands when he approaches. She's clutching a small red suitcase, dotted with tiny stars.

"Take me with you," Eadie Moon-Pie says.

Harn sits on the stairs. "I've nowhere to go," he says. "Not anymore."

"Let's go there together," she says.

Harn pulls Puppy from his coat, places him on the step. Puppy licks his hand, jumps in his lap, licks his face. Harn closes his eyes, leans against the railing. *Thump....* "In a little while," he says.

Eadie Moon-Pie sits, snuggles into Harn, closes her eyes, and waits.

CRSO

Puppy barks. Harn wakes. Puppy, still nestled in his lap, licks his face. The day is grey, the sun hidden behind a thick, foggy blanket of smoke and cloud. Harn nudges Eadie Moon-Pie.

"Morning," she says, rubbing sleep from her eyes.

Harn smiles. He can't remember the last time someone bid him a good morning. "Good morning," he answers.

Eadie Moon-Pie unlatches her suitcase, flips it open. She pulls out two bruised apples, and hands one to Harn. She places a few dry biscuits on the step beside Puppy, and Puppy eagerly gobbles them down.

Harn bites into the apple. "You'll take good care of Puppy."

She rubs the apple on her jacket, making it shine. "Yes," she says.

Harn scoops up Puppy and stands. Eadie Moon-Pie closes the suitcase, stands.

"Which way?" Harn asks.

Eadie Moon-Pie squints up at the charcoal sky, then scans the horizon. She points. "That way. South."

With Harn holding Puppy and Eadie Moon-Pie clutching her suitcase, they walk south. Shortly, they come to the river. Flies buzz along the scum-laden water surface. The air smells of rotted fish and sour milk.

"Follow the river?" Harn says.

Eadie Moon-Pie nods. "Yes."

They turn and head west, following the riverbank. They walk for several hours, then stop for more apples and biscuits. Eadie Moon-Pie pulls out bottled water, gives one to Harn, and hand feeds one to Puppy.

"How much stuff you got in there?" Harn asks.

"Enough," she says. "For now."

After their brief lunch, the three move on. The sun peeks through the clouds and smoke like a waking eye. The river bends and winds its way out of the city. Somewhere, on the outer edges of the city, they hear screeching and howling, mad laughter. It dissipates, the clouds part, and a red sun blazes. And suddenly the city is gone and they are in the country. Fields of tall grass stretch to the horizon. Crickets chirp and birds sing. The wind is cool mint and pine.

They follow the sun.

"Happy birthday," Eadie Moon-Pie says.

Harn looks at her. In the sun, her face is radiant. Briefly, his wire does a trip-hammer. *Thump-thump, thump-thump.* "Happy birthday, Eadie."

When the sun falls from the sky, they stop for a meager meal of dried nuts and bottled water. Puppy eats biscuits and chases butterflies. Harn stands. Pain slices his head. His vision blurs, goes black, then clears. He lifts a hand to his head, feels a lump above his ear.

Eadie Moon-Pie stands. Places a hand on his arm. Her touch is electric. "Are you okay?" she asks.

He looks down at her comforting hand, tries to smile. "Yes," he says. "I'm fine. Let's keep going, get a little farther, then try to find a place to stop for the night."

Eadie Moon-Pie nods, removes her hand from his arm. "Okay."

They walk on. The sun hangs like a beacon, then slips like a stone below the horizon, leaving a thin red band, pulsing. Soon, they crest a small hill and stop.

Thump....

Harn grabs hold of Eadie's hand, gazes at her. "This is it," he says.

There is a small ping in his head, a tiny, painful pinch. He closes his eyes and sees a constellation of fiery stars explode across his vision like some mammoth fireworks display. Another faint ping, a tearing, and a small "pop." The wire has snapped. That faint, omnipresent pulse disappears.

A broken heart.

Harn lies down in the tall grass. Puppy lies beside him, curls into his side. Eadie Moon-Pie gazes at the darkening sky.

It grows dark. The sky is a vast inky sea. The stars emerge, bright white gems winking open on a black canvas. Harn is staggered by its brilliance.

Eadie Moon-Pie lies down beside him. Puppy licks her arm. She slips a cool hand into Harn's hand.

"Thank you," Eadie Moon-Pie says, "for showing me the stars."

Harn smiles, closes his eyes. Stars wink across his lidded vision. Everything goes black.

He isn't afraid.

COMES A COOL RAIN

The laughing, giggling boy is throwing a doll lazily into the air and letting it drop onto the grey wool picnic blanket. A small, sardonic smile is stitched across the doll's face in black thread. *Swoosh.* The doll goes up, reaching its apex then tumbling lazily, end over end, and landing with a dull *thwump*.

Swoosh.

Thwump.

Swoosh.

Thwump.

The man looks up and through a mouthful of potato salad says, "Still playing with dolls, eh?" There is a twinkle in the man's eye, mirth in his voice.

"Hush, now," says the woman.

The boy smiles and sticks his tongue out at the father.

Then, black clouds and a fierce wind whipping tree branches. The scent of a summer storm — wet grass, moist earth and cool peppermint. And suddenly the rain, cold and hard.

The boy and his parents pack up their picnic and run laughing to the car.

Up one hill, down another. Past lush rows of green corn. Rich emerald and yellow hills whiz by like finger paint blurs.

"Please, slow down, Eric."

A nod of the head and a playful smile.

In the back seat the boy clutches the worn, ragged cloth doll. "It's like a rollercoaster, dad. The Flyer."

"Hmmm, yes. Yes."

Everywhere the green-brown earth, the black sky and pounding rain. The wipers flap-flapping, flap-flapping; the car fighting for purchase on the grey glistening ribbon of road.

A hand on the man's knee.

"Please, Eric."

"Sure, dear."

Easing up on the gas, a slight tap of the brake pedal and the car swerves to the left. Sharp intake of breath. A pull to the right and the car resumes its course.

"Whew, that was fun, dad."

Smiling, the man turns to son. "Was it, Joel?"

"Yeah! Do it again. Do it again."

The woman frowns. "Joel! Enough. Let your father get us home."

A pout. "Yes, mother."

Rain and wind and now hail--large and icy--batter the car. The world is green and black, obsidian, merging somewhere in the distant horizon.

Boom! Lightning crackles in the liquid sky.

Bright-eyed, the boy presses his milky-white face to the window. *Faster, dad,* the boy thinks. *Faster.*

The man strains at the wheel, forearms taut, white-knuckled. Perspiration rings his brow. Down a hill; hail chinking loudly off the hood. Up another hill and over the crest, the wind howling about them. Down, up, over. Down, up and over and too late, too late, the headlights of the truck, the squealing of brakes, the hiss of wet tires, the crunching of metal.

Too late but for the screams.

CRED

Joel, too old to play with dolls and too old for shedding tears, lay on his back on his bed, clutching a doll and crying silently. The tears formed little salty pools in his eye sockets. Mother was downstairs in the kitchen, rattling pans and banging cupboards, the busy noises and smells of the kitchen drifting up the heating grate in Joel's room. If he listened hard enough he could hear the click-click of the wooden clock mounted on the kitchen wall. And another sound, a low, somnolent rasping, like air leaking from a balloon, coming from his father's room.

And Joel wondered, like he did every day, if he had the courage to kill his father. His father wanted to die, he knew. Joel could see it in his eyes. Could sense it in the air like a gathering storm.

Joel placed the doll on his pillow and swung his legs over the edge of the bed, the left one hanging awkwardly, limp and useless. He placed his feet on the floor and pushed up, the right leg bearing most of his weight. He walked over to his mirror, the left leg swinging up and out in a circular motion. He grimaced.

Joel stood, leaning against the dresser, staring into the mirror, his hips throbbing in pain. He dabbed at his red eyes with a tissue. A flap of grey skin hung loosely from the spot where his right ear used to be.

Shortly, there was the sound of feet treading up the stairs and mother was standing in the doorway, drink in hand, the amber liquid swirling in the thick-cut glass.

Mother entered, coming over and sitting on the edge of the bed. She placed the drink down, picked up the limp doll and held it gently, her trembling fingers skimming lightly over the smiling face.

"Such a lovely, thing," mother said. "Always loved. Always cherished."

The window rattled and a shutter banged against the house. Mother sighed. "Guess I'll have to fix that soon." She looked out the window. The sky was darkening, black clouds gathering like lunatic locusts.

"You been crying again, Joel?"

"No."

"Good, cause big boys don't cry. Men don't cry. You ever see your father cry?"

Joel didn't answer and mother turned back to the doll.

"I remember when your father made this doll, Joel." The window was a dark mirror, reflecting back her face. "You were in my belly. Didn't know if you were an Ellen or a Joel. And so the doll," she said, inspecting it with eyes and hands, "neither boy nor girl. But smiling, happy." A weak smile curved her thin-lipped mouth. "Eric had said you'd be a happy child."

Rain was coming. Joel could feel the dull ache in his bones. He

39

shambled over to the window. Outside, the wind shrieked, shaking the house, and the loose shutter banged incessantly. A bird of prey wheeled in the darkening sky, inky-black against sooty, storm-laden clouds.

And Joel recalled another bird, many years ago:

He'd been playing outside in the hot August sunshine, a child of five or six. And, at the side of the house he'd found a bird. It lay in the grass, missing one eye, with a wing nearly torn off. With morbid curiosity he reached for it, thinking it dead. The greasy black bird squawked and pecked at him. It hopped up, the damaged wing flapping noisily, bounced a couple steps and fell over. A weak warble escaped its throat and Joel ran and got father, dragging him by the hand to the side of the house. Father wiped a hand across his brow and bent to inspect the injured creature. He prodded the bird with a black boot and it jumped up and wobbled a few paces away, fixing them with a cold feral stare from its good eye.

"Mind it doesn't leave, Joel," father said, disappearing around the house and returning with a shovel.

"Whatcha' gonna do, dad?" Joel asked. *"We can keep it. We can mend it."*

Father knocked the bird over with the shovel. *"It's beyond repair, son."* He trapped the thrashing thing between his boots, placing the point of the heavy shovel against the bird's throat. *"It's not a proper life, Joel. It's no way to live."* Father pressed down on the handle and the headless bird lay still. Joel blanched, sucked in his breath and stared wide-eyed at the lifeless creature. His mouth was moving but no words came from it. Later little Joel had helped dig the grave.

Joel gave his head a mental shake. For several minutes he watched the great bird circle and soar in the charcoal sky. Then he turned and gazed at mother.

Mother hugged the doll close and waited. Soon the first fat drops plinked against the window. The rain—the cool rain—was slapping against the pane and running down in blurry rivulets. Then came the tears, hot and salty as they washed down her reddening face and over her quivering lips.

Mother rocked the doll back and forth in a cradling motion, the same way Joel had seen her cradle and comfort father those first weeks back from the hospital.

"I never meant for it to be this way, Joel."

Joel wanted to speak, wanted to scream, couldn't. His chest was a tight fist, squeezing, squeezing.

Mother turned to him, her eyes red and puffy. "He was so good with his hands, Joel. Always making things. This doll, the swing set, the bookcase. Strong, gentle hands. Good for making things, touching. . . things. But now. . . " She choked back a sob, looked out the window. "Damn rain. Always the rain. It's not your fault, Joel. Wasn't your fault. It's the rain. I get all melancholy. Sorry, son."

Joel liked the rain, liked its cooling balm. He could teeter down the stairs and out the front door to lie on the wet grass, letting the rain wash over him.

"Can we g-go out?" Joel asked. "Into town, perhaps?"

Mother stared at him with dull, flat eyes. "No, almost dinner time, Joel. I have to feed your father. I can't leave him."

Joel frowned. "But he's fine, mother. It'll never change. He'll stay the same, whether we're here or not."

"Fine?," mother said. "You call that fine? And how would he feel, your father, your flesh and blood, knowing we were lollygagging all about the town. No, Joel, it won't do. You go if you want. Go if you must."

Joel sighed. "You're right, mother. I'll stay."

"Soon, Joel, soon. When you're a man."

Mother, face flushed red and still clutching the doll, stood and went out the door.

Joel listened. He thought he could hear his father's ragged breathing increase in pitch, as if he were excited or agitated.

Joel gritted his teeth, steeling himself, and lurched toward the door and out into the hallway. He hobbled down the short hallway, his leg windmilling painfully, and stopped at his father's room, gasping and panting for breath.

Mother was on her hands and knees, at the side of the bed. She was wiping up a runny brown liquid with a soiled rag. The room was hot and smelled of ammonia, vanilla and shit.

Joel gagged and mother looked up. "Damn bag broke again," she said, voice quavering slightly.

Joel stepped into the stifling room. He saw the ruptured colostomy bag on the bed, beside father's leg. "I'll help," he said, pitching towards the bed.

"No!" mother said, forcefully. "No. I'll do it, Joel. It's my fault. Should have checked him sooner."

"But, I. . ."

"Shush, now, Joel," she said, her voice softening. "It's okay. This was my decision. We were best prepared to care for your father."

Mother stood, apparently done cleaning though a reddish-brown stain was quite visible against the mint-green carpet.

"When you're older, Joel," mother said, her chest hitching, "when you've grown and become a man, you'll have decisions to make." She was near to tears again. "M-most times they will be simple things: Jeans or corduroys? Adventure or comedy? Soup or salad? But sometimes... sometimes... well, you'll see," she croaked. "When you're a man."

Mother turned and went to father's bed, sitting on the edge. Father, dressed in blue, striped pajamas, was propped upright against the headboard, his arms laying stiffly at his sides. His breath rasped and squeaked. The doll sat beside him.

Joel limped over to the other side of the bed and sat down, staring at his father.

Father's hair was growing back slowly in small, curly patches that sprouted willy-nilly atop his lumpy head. His eyes, once bright and sparkling, were unmoving flat black stones that stared dully into space. Father's ears and nose were bright pink nubs of hardened skin. The face was pink and shiny, the flesh stretched taut. The lipless mouth was pulled up in a grim rictus, a ceaseless wheezing emanating from that black maw. He looked as if he were made of pink plastic, as if he had melted.

Mother leaned forward with a bowl of oatmeal. It was thin and watery. She spooned some of the liquid into father's motionless mouth. Eric sputtered and gasped, shaking his head from side to side.

"Eric, time to eat," mother said. "Don't make things more difficult than need be."

Eric spit the gruel out, spraying the bed sheets and mother's face.

42

Placing the spoon in the bowl, mother hooked her arm around the back of Eric's head, her fingers grabbing hold of a nubby ear. "So be it, Eric," mother said. With her free hand she spooned some more oatmeal into Eric's mouth, forcing it past his clenched teeth. She set the spoon down and rubbed Eric's throat with the back of her hand. Joel saw the Adam's apple bob in a reflexive swallowing motion. Mother picked up the spoon, shoved it into the mouth and again rubbed the exposed throat. Over and over she repeated the procedure, holding tight to Eric's head, until the bowl was almost empty and oatmeal dribbled of Eric's chin onto his pajamas. Joel looked into father's eyes and, seeing nothing but hurt and tired resignation, looked away.

Mother placed the bowl down, wiped the chin clean with her bare hand, and pecked Eric on the cheek. "There, dear. That was your dessert." A small smile faltered on her lips. Eric, unmoving, gazed blankly at the ceiling.

"Now," mother said, "time to get another bag on you. Don't want any more accidents. Least none that can be avoided, anyhow." She was trying for levity, Joel thought, but her tone was dry.

"I'll do it," Joel said.

Mother's eyes flashed. "No, I can manage. I'll not burden you with this. Not yet, anyhow. For now, this is my responsibility." Then her eyes and voice softened. "You could get your father another pillow, though, son. He's looking a might unsettled."

Rain drummed against the window. Father's face gleamed with a sweaty sheen and a rattling noise escaped his mouth. Mother opened a drawer in the bedside table and drew out a fresh bag. She affixed the bag to the plastic tubing and covered it with the pajamas. "Should hold you a while," she said, patting Eric's leg.

With effort Joel lifted himself up and lurched toward the closet. He slid the door open, grabbed a pillow, and went around the other side of the bed to where mother sat. She was staring out the window. Outside, the sky was ashen and the rain had slowed to a steady mist.

"It's raining," mother said and Joel wondered who she was speaking to. "Rains a lot."

Mother stood, looked at Eric, her dull eyes roaming up and

down his thin body. She hugged herself with one arm, her free hand covering her mouth, quieting her soft whimpering. She looked at the grinning doll resting beside Eric. "You two aren't so different," she said. She trembled and shook, more tears filling her red-rimmed eyes, and hugged herself tighter.

Mother reached over and picked up a small plastic bottle from the table. She unscrewed the cap and, reaching forward, squirted a few drops into Eric's dry, unblinking eyes.

"I've got to check on our supper, Joel," mother said, turning. "You wash up, now, and come on down. There's fresh pie. And ice cream." She was out the door and gone, a faint odor of talcum powder and Jim Beam trailing in her wake. Joel thought he heard a moan escape her lips as she went down the stairs.

Joel stood over his father, his fingers clenching the soft folds of the pillow. He lumbered forward until his legs were touching the stained mattress. Except for the slight rise and fall of his chest, father was still. The eye drops had left little trails on his plastic face, as if he'd been crying. As if he could.

Joel regarded the glassy-eyed man with the melted face, the man who once was his father, and despair racked his body. He wanted to please his mother, make her happy. Wanted to be the man his father had been, the man his mother wanted him to be.

Joel's body shook and he whimpered like a frightened puppy.

Not a proper life, Joel.

Bending, Joel kissed his father on the forehead, and with trembling hands pressed the pillow against father's face. He watched the smiling doll and listened to the rain as he held the pillow fast. Joel shook and his resolve left, leaving him weak-kneed. He released the pillow and stared at father. Then, incredibly, father's eyes moved, staring warmly, almost pleadingly at Joel. A thick, garbled sound wheezed from father's throat.

"Pleesh!"

Please? thought Joel.

Joel dropped the pillow and turned. Father's hand snaked out and clutched at Joel's wrist, squeezing with a force Joel would have thought impossible. He shook free from father's grasp and shambled quick as he could to the door. He glanced back quickly, just long enough to see father's coal-black eyes staring coldly at him like that long ago crow.

Joel shuffled down the steps, out the front door and into the rain where no one could see him cry.

LIKE A STONE IN THE RIVERBED

The day was cool and grey and quiet. The world waited, holding an expectant breath. When the world exhaled, and a gust of chill wind carried dead, dry leaves tumbling along the gutter, Sheryl thought it sounded like water-worn pebbles rubbing and rolling over each other in a cool mountain stream. It was the same sad song.

Sheryl sighed, stepped into the A&P, and grabbed a cart. She pushed the shopping cart down the candy aisle. One wheel was bent, and squeaked like a cornered cat. She always seemed to get a broken cart. Another bad choice. Another broken part of her life. And Halloween was another reminder of that.

There was a sudden ache in her chest.

As Sheryl moved noisily down the aisle, she tossed in bags of tiny chocolate bars, gum, chips, licorice, and lollipops. All for naught, she knew. This year, as in previous years, there would be six or seven kids all told who would come to her door looking for a treat. Six or seven brave little souls. The rest would bypass her house. Though she'd lived there several years, she was the neighborhood stranger. The outsider. Because she kept to herself. Because she hadn't found anyone to give her heart to. There'd been a man once, Tim, whom she'd grown to love. And she tried to give him her heart, but he wouldn't take it.

Sheryl stared into the shopping cart. Too much candy. She'd end up eating the candy—all of it—over the next couple weeks, she knew. But she didn't care.

She wheeled the cart over to the checkout lane and dumped the candy onto the conveyor belt. She heard a faint noise, a sniffle, and glanced up.

The girl behind the cash register hurriedly wiped her eyes, blew into a tissue. She was a short, slight thing with black hair that hung like tattered ribbons. Her mascara had run, making her look like Alice Cooper.

Another sniffle and wipe of the nose. The girl took a deep breath.

"Cold?" Sheryl asked.

The girl looked up, revealing red-rimmed eyes. "What?"

"Do you have a cold?" Sheryl tried a faint smile. "Allergies?"

The girl looked down, shoved the used tissue into a pocket. "No. No. Nothing like that."

"What then?"

The girl straightened; stared up at Sheryl, shot her a venomous look. "I just found out I've lost my job. I've been fired. This is my last shift."

Sheryl blinked. "Oh. Oh, my. I'm sorry."

The girl's face softened. "Well, you asked."

"Yes," Sheryl said, "I did. I'm really sorry for you."

A terrible grin creased the girl's face. "Why? You don't know me. Nobody knows me. Don't go feeling sorry for me."

Sheryl nodded, was about to mumble "sorry" again but caught herself. She watched silently as the girl composed herself, bagged Sheryl's groceries and rang her through.

Collecting her bags, Sheryl walked out the automatic door into a grey world that seemed to stretch endlessly in all directions. The air was damp, and a faint thrum of electricity could be heard, as if Sheryl were standing under a large electrical pylon in a vast field. And, faintly, another sound reached Sheryl; shallow, gurgling, creek water flowing over cool dark stones. She remembered standing on the side of the small river, holding Tim's hand, watching the water cascade serenely down the creek bed; watching the gentle movements of the stones. One minute Tim was there, holding her hand. Then he was gone and heavy tears rolled down her cheeks. She stood there staring at the stones, so hard and smooth and cool and unfeeling. She watched them slowly roll and turn over with great effort. She envied them.

A bird shrieked, and Sheryl snapped from her reverie. She walked to her car, absently dumped the bags in the back, and climbed into the front seat. She sat and drummed her fingers along the steering wheel. Something the girl said kept repeating in her mind.

Nobody knows me.

Or me, she thought.

Sheryl sat in the car and waited, and waited. She was about to pull away when she saw the girl exit the store, a big olive-green burlap bag slung over a shoulder.

Something moved in her chest, paining her, making her wince. Sheryl pulled up to the curb, rolled the passenger side window down. Her heart knocked against her chest. She didn't quite know what she was doing. She should keep to herself. She couldn't get hurt that way.

"Can I give you a lift?" Sheryl asked.

The girl looked up and down the street, hesitating.

"I was in the store," Sheryl said. "You might not remember me."

"Yeah, I remember you."

"How about a lift, then? Can I drop you off somewhere?"

The girl shuffled her feet, hunched her shoulders. "You can drop me at the Y. I've got a room there. Until my money runs out."

The pain in Sheryl's chest was back. She tried to ignore it. "Y-You can come back to my place."

A blank stare from the girl. "You don't know me."

"Yeah, I know," Sheryl answered. She smiled weakly. "You told me that already." She reached over, pushed the door open. "Until you get sorted out. It's Halloween, after all."

The girl shrugged her shoulders. She threw the burlap bag into the back with the groceries, and clambered into the front.

The car pulled away from the curb and exited the parking lot. Sheryl could sense the girl staring at her.

"I'm Sheryl."

"Emma."

49

CR&O

Sheryl held the door open, letting Emma enter first. It seemed to Sheryl that it wasn't that long ago when Tim first opened this very door and ushered her into the house. And then she'd tried so very hard to give everything to him: her love, her heart. And it hurt. Lord how it hurt. But he refused her, and this same door had swung shut on them.

"Hey, I'm talking to you!"

Sheryl snapped alert. "Huh? Sorry. What did you say?"

Emma held the bags up. "Where do you want this stuff?"

Sheryl pointed. "The kitchen for now. We can put them in bowls and set them out for the kids a bit later."

Emma carried the bags into the kitchen, dropped them on the counter.

Sheryl entered the kitchen, went to the fridge and dug out two cans of cola. She popped the tabs, handed a can to Emma, then sat down and sipped at the soda. Emma sat across from her.

Sheryl leaned forward, her heart straining. "Why did you come?"

Emma blinked, pushed her can forward a couple inches, answered Sheryl with a question of her own. "Why are you running away?"

It was Sheryl's turn to blink. "What do you mean? I'm not running from anything?" She reached out, touched Emma's burlap bag. "You seem to be the one running."

"Am I?" Emma asked.

"Aren't you?"

"No. Well, I'm not running <u>away</u> from anything." Emma looked around. "I may be running <u>to</u> somewhere."

Sheryl smiled. She looked out the kitchen window. Bright orange leaves hung from the maple tree like little slivers of sun. She turned back to Emma. "And why do you think *I'm* running from something?"

Emma's eyes sparkled like the orange leaves. "Look around. This is your house, but you haven't made it your home." Her arm made a broad sweeping gesture. "It has no charm, no personality. It is devoid of any personal touches. No knick-knacks, no plants, no photos. If they were here, they are gone. A life erased."

"It's easier that way, Emma. I could leave, if I wanted. A person can get hurt," Sheryl said, "if they are not careful." She reached across the table, grabbed Emma's hand, gave it a gentle squeeze. Her heart rolled over in her chest like a stone in a riverbed. "I took a chance once."

Emma squeezed back, looked Sheryl in the eye. "And you're ready to take another chance." It was a statement.

CRISO

The day lengthened like a great grey elastic band pulled taut and tight. The wind pressed cold hands against the house, rattling windows, shaking doors, whispering secrets only it knew. Sheryl lit candles, tacked up decorations: witches, black cats, ghosts and bats. Emma poured candy into bowls, placed them on little tables near the front door.

On the kitchen table sat a large pumpkin the colour of rust and sunsets. Sheryl held a knife, enjoying its heft. She cut the top off the pumpkin, and it felt good, familiar. It had been so many years. A lifetime ago.

Emma was smiling, her hands dipping into the pumpkin and pulling out its pulpy, slimy innards. Sheryl dropped the knife and plunged her hands in. She grabbed some of the ropy entrails and mashed them in her hands, enjoying the cool and slick feel of it all.

Emma glanced at Sheryl. "What are you thinking?"

Sheryl blinked, half smiled. "I had a boyfriend."

"Me too."

"What happened?" Sheryl asked.

"I got pregnant. My parents kicked me out. I lost the baby. He left me. End of story."

"Some story."

"I just want what everyone wants." Tears pooled in Emma's eyes. "Family, friends. A normal life." Her eyes glanced about the room. "A place to call home."

51

Sheryl pulled her hands from the pumpkin, wiped them on a dish towel. She brought her hands up to her chest, cupped them over her heart. "I have something to give, to offer. Something precious. To the right person. I tried once. But he didn't want it. Didn't *need* it. See, it has to be given freely. But love isn't enough. I was wrong about that. Someone has to want it, *and* need it. You have to find the right person."

Emma grinned, wiped her hands then her eyes. "Yes." A whisper. "*Yes.*"

Sheryl stared at Emma, pain stabbing her heart.

Emma gestured to the living room. "I have something to show you."

Sheryl followed Emma to the living room. They sat on the couch. Emma reached into her burlap bag and pulled an item wrapped in tissue from it. She carefully unwrapped the tissue and held the object out for Sheryl. "Maybe we can put this up on a shelf. A personal touch. A start."

Taking the item, Sheryl winced then smiled. It was a snow globe, one of those cheap, plastic dome-shaped items filled with water and little sparkling pieces of paper that—when you turned it over—glittered and fell like winter's first gentle snow. Usually, they were emblazoned with words like *Niagara Falls*, and *The Grand Canyon*, with an appropriate scene encased in the plastic. This one, though, said *Baby's First Xmas*, and held a small baby dressed in pink and blue in a crib. Sheryl shook the globe, watched the snow slowly fall, watched the tiny crib rock back and forth, back and forth.

"I bought it," Emma said. "When I found out... well.... I thought it was cute."

"It is beautiful."

Emma twisted her hands in her lap. "It's all I have."

"It's enough." Sheryl stood, went and placed the snow globe on the mantel. She walked around the coffee table, and pulled Emma from her seat. They stood staring at each other. Sheryl brushed a clump of dark hair from Emma's face, her fingers lingering near Emma's soft mouth. "Come," Sheryl whispered, pulling Emma along the hallway, "It's my turn. I have something to show you."

In the bedroom, Sheryl sat Emma down on the edge of the bed. She kissed Emma tenderly, sweetly, on the lips, then straightened and began to unbutton her blouse. Emma started to lift her t-shirt but Sheryl stopped her.

"No, just me. I have something for you."

Emma watched as Sheryl unhooked the last button and shook free from her blouse. She undid the clasps of her bra, and slid it down her arms and off. Naked from the waist up, Sheryl stepped forward.

Emma gasped. Between Sheryl's breasts was a large, livid wound that pulsed and throbbed.

"Shhh," Sheryl placated. "It's okay. Really, it is."

"But, but --," Emma started.

"I'm ready, Emma. I am. To take a chance."

Sheryl hooked her fingers into the sides of the wound and tugged and tugged. When the wound gaped wide, she reached in and wrenched her heart free. It wouldn't cause her any more pain. She held the heart out to Emma in cupped hands. "Here. I give this to you freely. Everything is going to be all right now."

Emma could think of nothing else to do so she took the heart. It was heavy, wet, like a stone in a river.

CR80

The bowls were empty. All the candy was gone. Pirates and skeletons and mummies had paraded up to the door in an endless stream, cackling nervously. She hadn't thought to save herself any candy, but that was okay, there'd be more candy, more Halloweens. The candles burned down to their bases. The small flames flickered and danced, casting stark shadows on the walls. Emma finished carving the pumpkin. She gave it just the hint of a smile, a suggestion of happier times.

Sitting on the couch, Emma dozed. She could hear the wind outside, sighing, retreating. And she could hear something else; a dull beating sound, a shifting, tumbling noise like tiny tectonic plates moving and rubbing against each other. The sound pleased

53

her. She glanced up to the mantel, gazed at the snow globe, stared at the heart.

Emma closed her eyes and slept peacefully for the first time in a long, long while.

And when she woke at dawn to a new day, it was the finest, brightest morning she could recall.

RADIANT BOXER

Exceptin' for the bodies we buried, the day I meet Hector is like any other day in this damp and smelly city.

I'm buzzin', trippin' along, searching for a dark corner to lay my head, when I turn a corner into a wet alley and bump headfirst into Hector. Only I don't know his name is Hector; that's the first time I meet him, see, and don't know his name yet, and so I grunt and say "Whoa!"

The man-soon-to-be-known-as-Hector smiles. Big fella. Real big. Like one of them rasslers my daddy used to watch.

And I say "Whoa" again because there's nothing else to say, and on account of there be a dead thing in future-Hector's hands, and on account of all the blood. And I say "Whoa" because his face is covered in fleshy pale scars. Scars that pulse and glow like fat, white, wriggling maggots. His eyes are bright, bright. Like there's a light behind them, shining, trying to get out, dying to get out.

He grimaces. I take a step backward. He holds up the dead thing. An offering.

So I take it. 'Cause I'm not so stupid, see. Sure, I'm trippin' — just fuckin' blooming, actually — but I don't want to upset the big guy. He's got this big mother-fucking, shit-eating look. You know the kind. You do. The kind of mother-fucking, shit-eating look that says you better go along with whatever crazy mother-fucking, shit-eating idea he proposes. I can see it all over his fat face. I can read people. I'm quick that way. And I take the dead thing 'cause I can see right then and there that me and the big fella — Hector, only I still don't know his name yet — are going to be fast friends. Yes, fast friends. I can see it in his big, liquid eyes.

55

Exceptin' I don't need friends, fast or not.

So I take the bloody, furry thing and he smiles blankly. Speaks. "Hector." And that's when I learn his name.

Hector.

I'm quick that way.

It's a dog, the dead thing. A black and bloody mess. I don't blame Hector. I don't. We all get a little crazy sometimes. Even me. Probably a stray, anyway. Like me. Like me and my new friend Hector, here.

"Hector," he says again, still smiling blankly, his voice a gargle of ground glass. I can tell he isn't much for words. "Pierre," I say, chuckling, and pointing to my chest. Pierre, I think. That's fuckin' rich.

Once, long ago, I was Peter. Just Peter. Plain ole' Peter. But that was a different time, a different life. Or Pete. L'il Pete as my daddy would say. L'il Pete as he beat me with his belt, then, later, with his fists. Mr. former Golden Gloves. *Left right right. Jab jab.* The only time daddy ever seemed truly happy was when he was in the ring, beating on someone, or beating on me. He was all smiles. Smiles and knuckles. And always Momma, after, cooing and placating, saying I mustn't cry, telling me it was love. Daddy was filling me with love. *You have to know pain to learn love.* And all that love would grow, and spill out of me.

Yeah, right. Love. Love is painful, let me tell you.

Hector looks at me all quizzical like. Big wet puppy eyes. Looks like he's going to cry. Then he is crying. But he's still smiling. Crying and smiling. Ker-rist!

I put the dead dog down, fish an old handkerchief from my soiled pocket and press it into Hector's hand. Big hands on the big fella. Hands that could snap a dog in two.

Hector blows his nose. Right in my hankie. Then he starts rubbing the handkerchief all over his arms and hands, trying to clean the blood. Ker-rist! He's a real mess. Smiling, he hands me the hankie. I drop it to the ground.

Must be new on the block, Hector. I never seen him before. Hard to miss Frankenstein, here. Hard to miss him anywhere, come to think. Can't have been on the street long. Big fellas don't stay big for long. He'll be wire thin by winter. Those scars, though. They ain't going anywhere. My daddy had similar scars. I guess I got some too. You just can't see 'em.

So, 'cause I'm still trippin', still looking for a place to lay low, I start to leave. Real slow like. Just walking, eyes straight ahead, fixed down the dank alley. Slow 'cause I don't want to upset my new friend, Hector, here. Don't want to startle the big fella.

And I saunter, real slow like—slow as I can while hopped up— past greasy cardboard boxes, past mangy cats, past garbage bags, and dumpsters, and large oily puddles. I see a dead pigeon, a black and white speckled thing, twig legs sticking straight up in the air cartoon-like.

I see Effie, stick-thin woman with her pregnant belly. My racing heart twists, feels like a knife is shoved between my ribs. Looks like her kid has dropped. Any day now, I think. Damn! Effie said the kid is mine. Damn! Woman's been with everyone on this block, and half the next block. How does she know a thing like that? How? Damn! When she sees me she waves, and what passes for a smile, but is more a frown, crosses her face. Some women look real fine when they're pregnant. Not Effie. But she's a good kid, really. Sweet, kinda. Innocent, too. Telling me all about how her kid is gonna grow up and do good things; have a good life. Telling me how I'm gonna be her guardian angel. Oh, man! And I help her out when I can, seeing as how she's got a young 'un to care for. Sometimes I think that me and Effie could... well... shit, I dunno, be together. You know, for companionship. That sorta thing. But then I come to my senses, remember that I don't need no friends.

I get halfway down the alley when I hear a noise behind me. Shuffling and sobbing. I turn, and Hector is there, his round face twisted in pain, his eyes screwed shut, tears leaking past the closed eyelids. His mouth opens and closes, making blubbering sounds. He's clutching that damn dead dog, holding it tight to his chest, crying like a goddam baby. Hector is shaking, and it is like a rumbling mountain.

Hector is upset.

Yeah, I'm quick that way.

I feel like smacking him in the face. Feel like smacking the shit out of the big pansy. 'Cause now I'm down. The bloom is gone. And Frankenstein is following me around like a lost puppy. Yeah, I know, fast friends and all that, but sometimes a man needs his space.

So Hector is shoving the dog at me again, pushing it into my chest. He's blubbering some nonsense, and making funny gestures with his arms. Then I get it, because I'm quick: He wants to bury the dead dog. Wants *me* to help him.

Fuck!

But we're fast friends, now, me and Hector. Plus, being the quick sorta fella I am, I can tell Hector ain't gonna let me be. So I carry the damn dog up the alley—trying to ignore the garbage and the cats and Effie—across the street, past the park and into the woods. Hector follows, lumbering and wheezing. He's a good Frankenstein.

In the woods I find a big branch, a thick one, and hand it to Hector. He stares at it, dumbfounded, holds it tight in his meat-sausage hands. For an instant there I think he's gonna take a swing at me, Barry Bonds-like. Yeah, Barry Bonds. I read the papers. Guys like him are doing more junk than me. But they can afford it. Don't gotta scrounge outside the liquor store.

I grab another pointed branch and begin clawing at the dirt. We must be a sight, the two us. Soon we've got a hole big enough for the dog. That damn dead dog! So I kick the dog, shove it into the hole with my booted foot. I'm not really mad at the dog, really. Mad at my situation, is all. And we fill the hole in, Hector and me. Fill it in good and fast, 'cause the light is leaving, and, truth be told, I don't wanna be in the woods when it's dark. The woods always kinda spooked me. Yeah, I got me a big pointy stick and all, but, fuck, I don't know—it's too damn dark. Give me a dark alley any day.

And off we go again through the woods, past the park, across the street into the alley. Home. I don't see Effie anywhere. I hope she found a warm spot. She's been real weird of late. Talking nonsense. Talking shit. Telling me stories about angels and souls and whatnot. Telling me she loves me. Right! Ain't that fuckin' precious? Why does she gotta talk like that? Huh? I get the feeling she *knows* me. Knows about my daddy, and his knuckles, and how they filled me with love. And she wants some of that love. And I... I dunno. I just remember momma saying you have to know pain to learn love. I guess Effie knows pain. I guess we all do. Shit! Getting knocked up musta made Effie loopy.

It's quiet exceptin' the occasional howl from a cat and Hector's heavy breathing in my ear. Looks like the big fella ain't goin' anywhere fast. Got me a friend.

The knot in my stomach tightens. Time to eat something. I thread my way through some narrow back alleys, over to Chan's. Hector follows. But there's nothing at Chan's, exceptin' some cats fighting over old Egg Foo Young. At Luigi's, two blocks over, we have better luck. There's some lasagna and bread and a bunch of those giant meatballs you usually only see on Saturday mornin' cartoons. I see some leftover salad, too, but it is a runny, soggy mess. I have standards, you know.

Me and Hector sit down against the wall and eat. I slip the bread in my pocket. Effie could use it, I think. Eating for two and all that.

"Good," Hector says, smiling through mouthfuls of garlic bread and lasagna. He's got blood and dirt and pasta sauce smeared all over his face. And those scars on his face, those nubs, are wriggling and shining. He's some fuckin' sight, I tell ya.' Some fuckin' sight.

Done eating, I stand. Hector stands, grins at me like a crazy-ass mother. The wind bites into me. Cold. I pull the collar on my thin jacket up. And I wonder about Effie. Wonder how she's doing. Wonder if she found a warm spot tonight. Ker-rist! I shake my head. Why do I give a shit.

I start down the alley, hands in pockets, shoulders hunched. I don't hear anything. I don't hear Hector's heavy footsteps, his heavy breath. I turn, see the big fella standing, throwing punches. Punches at nothing. He's shadow boxing. *Left left right. Jab jab roundhouse uppercut.* His arms are flying, whirring. *Left right jab. Jab jab right uppercut.* Good footwork. Good balance. Kid's a natural. A boxer. Not a rassling dude. A boxer. That explains the scars. Though that don't explain why they glow, why they move like dying worms.

So I watch him awhile, fists like blurry sledgehammers, cutting through the air. Watch him dance like that Ali fella. Then I whistle and he stops, comes trotting over like a puppy. He's grinning broadly, face full of scars, all glowing like a jar full of fireflies. I ain't never seen anyone so happy. And, for a second, I'm happy for him. I head down the alley, checking over my shoulder to see if Hector is following. He is. And I again wonder why I even give a shit.

By now I'm starting to get that edge back. Starting to get a little antsy. Jumpy. I need a little something something to take the world away.

Hector smiles, his face radiant. He bends, picks something from the ground. It's a bird. A dead pigeon. The black and white one I saw earlier. Ker-rist! Fuck him and his dead things. I don't need this shit. Yeah, I know, I know, fast friends and all that.

He's still smiling. He's clutching the pigeon in one hand, holding it up to his face, and his other hand is rubbing, squeezing, pulling at his scars. His fingers probe his face; sink into the white nubs, pry open a scar. Shit! White light spills out, bathes the pigeon. Hector, still smiling, fingers digging deep, pulls open another scar, then another. Bright beams of light, like tiny flashlights, leak from his face. A halo of white light covers the pigeon. And Hector, face plastered with that Frankenstein smile, moves his head real slow like—trance-like—bathing the dead thing in soft white light. Then the pigeon stirs. A leg twitches, a wing flutters, and the bird is up and flying away. Fuckin' flying away.

"Whoa!" I say. I'm trembling now, shaking like a cold skinny dog. Hector walks over, grinning. His face is pale. All the light has left his face, and his scars lay dull and dormant, like dead things. Fuck! Hector and his dead things.

Shivering, teeth chattering, I step back. I'm trembling like a newborn. Like a junkie. Hector starts into his routine, his tree-limb arms spinning like dervishes. *Left right right left jab hook.* His face begins to take on colour, begins to glow, to *radiate. Jab jab hook uppercut.* It's like he's winding up, recharging. The scars begin to pulse and wriggle. Hector stops boxing and pushes on the scars, peeling back the hardened flesh. His face is leaking light again. Then he's got me by the shoulders, and he's waving his head as if he's grooving to some internal soundtrack, and the light is so warm, so warm, and I'm drifting, drifting, and that antsy edge just leaves me, washes away like leaves in a rain gutter. And I'm not shaking anymore, not craving a hit. All I feel is love, nothing more.

Just love.

And I remember Momma telling me how you had to know pain to learn love. I could picture Hector, in the boxing ring, taking blow after blow. Absorbing all that pain. The kinda pain that a quick fix won't take away. And all Hector's pain musta built up, and turned into something else. Turned into love, just like Momma said. And that love was spilling forth, shining out. Fuck! A radiant boxer.

Hector grins his mother-fuckin' grin. "Better," he says.

I nod, smile, hug him close.

Suddenly, I want to find Effie. I want to give her the bread. I want to give her a big hug, tell her it's gonna be all right. Everything's cool. Everything's good.

That's when I hear the shrill wail, the lonesome cry. A baby's cry.

I go racing up the alley. Hector follows, feet clomping, breathing hard. We turn the corner and there's Effie, seated, head leaning against the rough brick, eyes closed, skin pale pale. She's holding something in her lap, and I know it's her kid, her baby. She had the baby. In the alley, dammit!

We reach Effie and the baby. There's blood everywhere. Too much blood. The baby is wailing, shrieking; but Effie's eyes are still closed. She's sheened in sweat and her skin is the colour of sour milk. And she smells like curdled milk. Hector starts into his bit, his routine, throwing furious hooks and jabs and uppercuts. His face, his scars, begin to glow. He stops, grunts, then pries at the scars, sinks his fingers deep into the hardened nubs of flesh and pulls, pulls, until bright white light shoots out. Hector picks up the naked, blood-slicked baby, holds it tight near his face and lets the light dance over the baby. Soon, the baby is quiet, still, and content.

I'm trying to wake Effie, trying to get her attention. I shake her, squeeze her hand, yell in her ear. But she doesn't move, doesn't stir. There's too much fucking blood! Hector hands me the baby. I look around and see Effie's backpack. I fish around inside the pack and find a knitted shawl. I wrap little Effie in the shawl, and rock her gently in my arms, cooing, like Momma used to coo.

Hector stands over Effie, recharging, throwing punches at the air. His hands are a blur. His head shines, making light. All I see is a corona, a halo of white, like a crown. Then he's got her in his tree-limb arms, and he's throwing light on her, all over her, but Effie is limp and bloody, and I recall the dead dog. The dumb dead dog we buried in the park. But Hector continues to try and fill her with love, with life, letting the light wash over her body, until, finally, the last bit of love leaks meekly from his face and winks out. He looks at me, his face quivering, and begins to sob, to blubber like a baby. Love and regret stab me, and I cry, nodding toward the street.

So Hector lifts Effie, throws her over his shoulder. And we start walking down the alley, toward the park.

To dig another hole.

'Cause even angels can't save everyone.

CR80

Later, back in the alley, Hector by my side, little Effie bundled securely in my arms, I remember the bread. I fish it from my pocket, take a bite, and hand it to Hector. He pulls off a hunk, smiles, and hands the bread back. I stare at the stale bread, take another bite, and try not to cry.

Little Effie smiles, gurgles, and her face is radiant.

THE SIMPLE SOUND OF DEAD TREES SINGING

(with C.S. Fuqua)

Errol Beason rocked slowly, letting the chair's curved runners roll over the warped hardwood.

Berrummpp-berrummpp.

The battery-powered radio squawked and hissed static. Occasionally he heard the KMOX announcers calling the game between the Cards and Cubs,

(...strike three, and Sosa is caught looking to end the inning...)

then something else,

(*...Jimmy. I love you, Jimmy...*)

but then it would fade and peter out, leaving a steady droning buzz.

Jimmy had liked baseball, Errol recalled.

Errol brought the rocking chair to a halt.

Berrummpp.

He stood, stretched the kinks out of his bone-weary body, and crossed the room to the door. Quite suddenly he felt like an old man, felt out of sorts and lost.

Errol opened the door and stepped outside. He hopped off the short porch and sauntered along the path into the woods. He hoped he wouldn't get lost like last time.

The hot summer wind whipped through the pines, sighing and moaning. If you cocked an ear, tilted your head in just the right direction, it sounded like singing. Sweet and sad and low. Dead trees, Errol noted. Thin and skeletal fingers bending and snapping like dry bone in the summer breeze. Not a pleasant sound, but comforting in a way Errol couldn't quite understand.

Errol, shoulders hunched, hands shoved deep in his pockets, continued along the forest's worn footpath. Late afternoon sunlight filtered through the uppermost canopy, little spotlights dotting the path, showing the way. Dust motes danced in the golden light. Specks of diamond.

I ought to get back to the cabin, Errol thought, then chuckled cheerlessly. Get back for what? To sit and rock in the corner chair like a ragged old man, the static of an old radio his only company? To sit and think about how things could have been? To pace the tiny room in the tiny rented cabin and wonder how it all went so terribly wrong?

The dead trees bent and sang in the wind. It was a sound like stressed wood, Errol thought. A simple sound. The sound Jimmy's rope had made, hanging from the thick wooden beam of the family room when Errol had come down to find his son dangling at the end of the tether, swinging in some phantom breeze, the wood creaking, groaning, creaking, singing. . . . How long had he been there? The body still had heat.

Errol's pace quickened.

The image of Jimmy's shoes twirling above the overturned chair twisted through his mind. Two black-and-white sneakers at the end of denim-clad legs, spinning slowly. Not from some ghost wind, but from the weight of Jimmy's body. And Errol knows that it hasn't been long, that his son may have kicked the chair from under his feet only a few minutes ago, but minutes are as good as days because he's too late. He had started down once before, started down and turned back for a different shirt, something not so heavy.

He doesn't dare look up into his dead son's face because that's not how he wants to remember him. So he sits—actually pulls a chair over, eases his trembling body into it—and stares long and hard at the slowly spinning shoes. Hears the horrible sound of creaking, singing wood. Many things, he now realized, were made of dead trees. Had they always sung to him? Had he just ignored them until now?

64

Lately another picture has been forming in his mind, intruding upon his thoughts and dreams: a dark form swinging silently in a bare, wan room. Errol's eyes pan slowly upward to gaze at his own impassive face staring back down at him. His eyes are cold and accusing. It's not an unpleasant sight. Fitting. Right.

Errol shakes his head, breaking the reverie.

Something lay in the path ahead. Errol moved closer, bent and picked it up. A nest of leaves and grey twigs, brittle and as dead as his marriage. It crumbled in his hands.

Wendy had been at the funeral, of course. She hadn't spoken to him, but he saw it all in her eyes — the condemnation, the anger.

And who could blame her? If he was any kind of a father, his son would still be alive. What kind of father was he that his own flesh and blood couldn't talk to him about his troubles?

Errol shuddered. Something moaned — him or the trees, he couldn't quite tell. The chill wind continued to blow.

Errol hugged himself, wiped the back of his hand across a teary cheek, kicked at the hard-packed ground. *He could have told me*, he thought. *He should have come to me. I would have listened.*

It wasn't Errol's fault. Or so his friends, relatives and doctors had told him. He was a good man, a good father.

Yeah, Errol mused, *a good father with a dead son.*

If only he'd hugged Jimmy more often, told him how proud he was of him. Told him he loved him.

I love you, son.

Even now it wasn't an easy thing to acknowledge. Too little, too late.

"Why is it so *hard* for fathers to tell their sons they love them?"

"Macho bullshit. That's why."

Errol stopped short, startled by the voice. He looked up sharply, never expecting to find the girl. Young and pretty in a plain sort of way, dishwater hair pulled back into a ponytail, slender and unremarkable. She sat on a low branch of a dead pine, idly kicking her thin legs out, letting them swing back lazily. She had big brown liquid eyes. He guessed her age at fifteen or sixteen. A bit younger than Jimmy.

"Wh-what did you say?" Errol asked.

65

The girl smiled. "Macho bullshit." She shrugged, made a popping sound with the gum in her mouth. "It still isn't cool for men to show their feelings. Stupid, if you ask me."

Errol glanced away, avoiding her gaze. Was she mocking him? "Did I speak aloud?"

The girl nodded.

Errol sighed, felt his face warm. "Sorry," he sighed. "I didn't think anyone else was out here."

"You were wrong," the girl said. She stopped kicking her legs, leaned forward, hands gripping the branch to either side of her for balance. "Betty."

Errol shuffled forward, held out his hand. She reached down, but it was too far. She smiled, straightened. "Errol," he said, dropping his hand.

"Nice name," she said. "Like *error*."

His gaze narrowed sharply. Was she teasing again? She closed her eyes, tilted her head to the sky. Sunlight filtered through the branches to streak her face in shards of stark light. The breeze rattled the leaves around her, and Errol felt the chill again. He looked away, thought about leaving.

"My parents..." the girl started. Errol stopped, twisted his neck for another look up at the girl. He felt slightly uncomfortable below her like this, as if she were some kind of nymph he'd stumbled on. As if this pale, thin thing would pounce on him.

"My parents," the girl said again, "they *always* tell me how much they love me. So what?" She snapped her gum. "Doesn't mean sweet fuck all. A hug would be nice. Or a smile."

Errol rolled his shoulders uncomfortably, didn't care for the familiarity with which this girl spoke. The girl looked down at him. "Listen," she said, eyes widening, the smile playing with her lips. "If you listen close enough, you can hear them saying it now: I love you, Betty. I love you." Her smile tightened, it seemed to Errol, just enough to resemble a snarl.

Errol coughed. "Your parents are gone?"

The girl's lips puckered and she gave a shrug, looked back up through the tree toward the sky. "Yeah. They're *gone*. Dead. Doornail dead."

66

Somewhere overhead, a crow cawed. The wind ebbed, the singing softening.

"I'm sorry," Errol said.

The girl grinned. "*You* didn't kill them." She looked down. Then, playfully: "Did *you*?" Before he could respond, she shifted on the limb, seating herself side-saddle, and said, "Shouldn't apologize for something you know nothing about."

Tears, inexplicable tears, formed in Errol's eyes. He half-turned away so she wouldn't see. The urge to flee welled up. He felt exposed, vulnerable, and it was not a feeling he cared for, not from this girl, not from his wife, not from Jimmy. *From Jimmy.* He drew a heavy breath to steel himself. When he glanced up, the girl's gaze met his.

"Car accident," Betty said. "Late December, and if you were from around here, you'd know how treacherous the winter roads can be. Happened not too far from here, on Highway 50, just down the road a ways. We were heading to a Christmas concert at my high school. The snow was heavy."

"You were in the car?" he asked, his voice sounding strangely subdued to him.

"Yup. The wind was howling. Couldn't see three feet in front of us. We went off the road and hit a hydro pole. Killed them both. Simple as that."

Yeah, Errol thought, *simple. Unplanned. Not like buying a thick, corded rope, making a loop (thank you, Boy Scouts), throwing it over the beam, anchoring one end, getting a chair, stepping up, putting your neck in the noose, leaning, rocking the chair... .*

Simple.

He cleared his throat, a nervous little cough. "But you... Were you hurt?"

She rolled her eyes, cocking her head to one side in dismissal. She shifted on the branch. Her jeans, he now noticed, were ripped at the knees, frayed around the seams, and her sneakers old, heels worn on the outer edges, the way his running shoes would wear, as if he were always fighting the road to get inside, to find safe haven... He let the thought go. There are no safe havens.

"You look familiar," she said. "What's your son's name?"

"My son?"

"Yeah, Einstein," she said, the taunting little smile returning.

Errol's throat tightened. He felt anger rising. What right did she have to tease him? "Jimmy," he muttered. He gazed at the ground. The wind stirred again. Leaves rattled around his feet, flipping carelessly across the forest floor. The song hummed around him.

"Beason?" the girl chirped.

Errol nodded.

"Your son's Jimmy *Beason*?" She laughed. "I know Jimmy." Then, as suddenly as the lilt appeared in her voice and the anger raged in Errol's mind, Betty slumped sadly, her mouth drawn and wrinkled. "Guess it's my turn to say sorry," she said.

Errol wanted to say *forget it*, but the words couldn't get past the lump in his throat. He grimaced and spat, shoved his hands deep into his pockets; saw his own face in his mind's eye, black and puffy, rope rising from his broken neck. A picture of justice, he thought bitterly. He'd lived most of his life, most of the years allotted to a person, and what kind of life had it been? What had he done? Worked. Married. Divorced. Somewhere in there, he'd fathered a son. That could have been the highlight of his otherwise worthless life. Was that worthlessness the reason his son had been taken? Why Jimmy? Why Jimmy, for god's sake, why?

Errol straightened, craned his neck for a better look at this girl. "So you know about Jimmy?"

She smiled that feral smile. "Yep." She shrugged. "I know a lot of things."

Errol looked down, tight-lipped, saw leaves tumble across his shoes. She probably met Jimmy up here one summer, he thought. A girlfriend? Just another thing Jimmy never talked about? Just another...

"You okay?" Betty asked. "Want to talk about it?"

Errol shook his head. He glanced away. "I'm not sure you'd be the one I'd choose if I did," he said coldly. The light was fading to a murky twilight. Silver-limned branches swayed and sang in the summer air. Abruptly, he started away. "Look, it was nice and all...."

A dull thump behind him, and Errol turned to see Betty standing in the path, hands on hips, defiant and also vulnerable. "I never said it either," she called. "Who knows why people don't say the words?" She dropped her head momentarily in acceptance. "Maybe words don't matter sometimes. Fuck, really. Words are just words."

The wind whistled through the trees. Errol stiffened. It sounded like a scream.

The girl turned and started off on a run, ducking and weaving through the undergrowth, leaving Errol under the tree, taken off guard, staring after her. "Hey!" he shouted. "Hey!" And then he was running as well. If he could catch her, if he could only catch her....

Leaves slapped him, branches raking across chest, legs, arms. He lost sight of the girl. She was like a fox; quick and sly and elusive. A trickster, he thought. He stopped, held his breath, heard the muffled pounding of feet over the pounding of his own heart. Heard branches snapping and, then, something that made the hair on his neck stand: a high trill laugh.

Anger raged within again. She *was* mocking him. She'd mocked him the entire time. Like Jimmy.

Jimmy.

Or was it the other way around?

He pushed on, brushing away branches that clawed and brambles that bit. It grew cold. Errol's breath steamed and fogged in front of him, and, vaguely, his mind whispered, *But it's summer.* The wind pushed and pulled, frigid fingers buffeting him. Wet snow fell, suddenly, in heavy white blankets, scratching at his face and hands. Errol came to a bewildered stop. "Impossible," he whispered. "It's *summer*." The world was a swirling white vortex. Slowly, unconsciously, Errol hugged himself, fear spreading through his mind like an insane scream. He didn't know which way to go, so he chose a spot and stepped forward.

A road, the side of a road to be precise, black pavement visible in patches in the snow. Errol turned, looked behind him. A fog-white wall pulsed and fluttered. He could see no paths, no breach where he'd come through. He turned dumbly back to the road. Dusk. A sodium light shone weakly from a black pole, throwing pale light on the slick road. Flakes like dust motes rushed through the light in some mad dance. Specks of diamond. The snow thickened, falling steadily, burying the road, the poles and the hanging wires under smothering white.

A sound reached Errol's ears. He turned, watched as a car crested the small hill and slipped down the other side, gaining speed.

The tiny car swerved awkwardly, skidded to the side and smashed into the wooden pole with a heaving crunch and groan, the sound of dead trees singing.

Smoke and steam coughed from under the car's crumpled hood. Amongst the wreckage something stirred, slipped from the back seat and scampered away.

Errol stuttered forward, tears pooling in his eyes, glistening into ice on his cheeks. His leg buckled, and he went to his knees as snow raged into his eyes. He squeezed his eyes shut, again, and the snow was gone. So were the road and the twisted car. All that remained was a lone wooden pole with a weak, wan light.

Something groaned, creaked. Errol looked up, up, craning his neck, shielding his eyes from the light atop the pole. A body twisted in the wind.

But his eyes wouldn't look away. The body turned, spun to face him. Errol blanched, shook. And he was back in his cabin, gazing up to a far dark corner, at himself, at his lifeless body.

A hand clasped his shoulder, jarring him with fright. He scampered to the side, a whimper escaping.

"It's okay. Really." Betty smiled at him.

Wind touched his face. Leaves scattered around him. The cabin vanished. He was in the woods, the scent of pine stinging his nose, his eyes, the heat of summer whistling in the song of trees.

"Wh–what...?" he stuttered.

Betty shook her head slowly, her expression of acceptance, consolation. "Make your peace, Errol, then move on."

"The accident," Errol rasped. "You couldn't have survived..." Then he remembered the dark form slipping into the night and his eyes widened.

"I didn't survive." She grinned. "Not really."

Again, anger welled. "Who are *you* to tell me what to do about *my* son?" he growled. "How does anyone make peace when they've been so wrong?"

She laughed. "I didn't say make peace with Jimmy. It's *yourself* you have to deal with now. Everything else will fall into place. Find your own way."

Errol's hands trembled, and he felt desperately cold in this summer heat.

"Don't worry about Jimmy," she said. "He tried. Too hard."

Errol looked up.

"You started down once, but you went back. You went back to change your shirt. That's the thing about life. There are so many random choices we make. One choice leads to a different future from another. One choice can save a life, one destroy it, one avoid it, and we usually never know. Jimmy made a choice. *His* choice."

The trembling encompassed his entire body, and he felt as though he would collapse completely.

"Remember?" Betty said softly. "Do you remember Jimmy *ever* telling *you* 'I love you, Dad.'"

Errol's chest hitched, and he could not stop the sobs that came. "Jimmy," he cried. "Jimmy."

"Another choice. A different path. Words." Betty bowed her head and took a step back. She half-turned, spreading thick undergrowth and paused. "Everybody finds his way eventually. People take chances; people make chances. And you deal with it. Words are words, Errol. Don't dwell on what was and wasn't said. Move on."

She slipped through the opening in the bushes. The bushes shuddered closed behind her, swallowing her. Errol heard leaves crackling and breaking, rushing away under the feet of animals.

The wind blew, dead trees trembling in their chorus. Errol slowly regained control, wiped his face dry, and stood. He wandered without direction, noting dead trees subconsciously, sighing with their song, trying to ignore the vision of his slack, indifferent face and cold hard eyes staring down at him from the taut rope.

Finally, without realizing his direction, Errol found himself back at the cabin.

71

He pushed open the door, went inside. Errol shuffled over to the rocking chair and collapsed into it.

Berrummpp-berrummpp.

His radio was still on, the batteries seemingly lasting forever. The Cards and Cubs were playing. Something stirred in a far dark corner.

Errol cocked an ear, listened. He heard dead trees singing.

He rose and stretched. Dust motes sparkled in a shaft of morning light. Specks of diamond. He ambled across the room and out the door. He stepped off the porch and into the woods, listening for the song. The woods were dark, and he sometimes got lost in them.

Today, Errol thought. Maybe today I'll find my own way.

A PLACE OF STONES
AND THORNS

It was His will.

Mother died, and it was His will.

ෂ෨ඏ

I see a mitten in the dirt. It is brown. Everything in the Camps is brown or grey; the earth, the tents, my clothes, my skin.

I pick the mitten up. Perhaps it wasn't always brown. Perhaps it is just dirty. I picture it green or purple—colours I've seen in books. When father had books.

I put the mitten on, rub it against my cheek. It pleases me.

I've never had a mitten.

It is hot today. It is hot every day. There is no need for mittens, obviously. Perhaps people in the northern Camps wear mittens. It is colder up north, near the Great Lakes. Or so I hear. I think, years ago, I read about the Great Lakes. In father's books. Or he read them to me. Now, like books, the Great Lakes are just legend. Stories told around campfires. Stories told at Sermon.

At Sermon one night they told a tale of a large western Camp, once the largest western Camp, far, far to the west, where land meets water. They told us how this Camp incurred His wrath. They told us how the land shook and the earth heaved and the Camp fell, twisted and broken, into the water.

It was His will.

73

The sun is high and bright in the blue sky. Such a pretty sight, the sun and the sky. Like a golden coin rippling in a clear mountain stream. A scene mother would have enjoyed. A scene she would have loved to paint.

I still wear the mitten. It feels strange to have my fingers covered, to flex my hand. A thumb and one big finger. Like an animal. I bend, pick up a stone, grip it tightly. I'm an animal.

For the past several nights I've been staying with Choi and his family. Choi is my friend. They have a comfortable tent. After mother died the council put me in a communal tent. But it is large and lacks intimacy. I will stay with Choi's family until they tire of me.

For breakfast I ate two apples. I went to the grove and picked them, climbing to the uppermost branches which bear the sweetest, sun-drenched fruit. I peeled the apples and saved the skin. Later, tucking my mitten in a pocket, I drank with cupped hands from the lake. Then I went with Choi's family to morning Sermon. After Sermon we will eat lunch. Then the Community will gather at the cross on the high hill.

And we will Pray.

CRED

Always, the thorns cut my hands.

For lunch I ate berries from a prickly bramble bush. The bush is far from Camp. Mother showed me the bush. She discovered it one day while walking. She said to me, "Grace, though this is a place of stones and thorns, there is beauty still." Mother loved beauty. That's why she named me "Grace." She said I was full of grace and beauty. I was her amazing Grace.

I did not go with Choi and his family to the high hill. I did not go to Prayer. I hope they do not miss me. I will make an excuse, feign an illness.

Today the berries were sweet and juicy, their blood-juice running off my chin to stain grey stones. They looked like painted rocks, and that made me think of mother. So, careful that no one was around, I used my bleeding fingers to paint on other rocks; dogs, cats,

74

families. After I'd admired their beauty, I took the rocks to a nearby stream and washed them clean. I left them in the cool, clear water. They looked like polished bone.

Always, the thorns cut my hands. My hands felt as if they'd received a thousand cuts, so I put my mitten on the sorest hand and it felt better.

Father, dear father, was the first to tell me about the thousand cuts. "Ling Chi," he called it. Information he read in an ancient text. The death of a thousand cuts. They string you to a tree, or a cross, and carve away small pieces of your flesh, your skin, until you bleed out.

Sated from the berries, I slipped away to the cave. It is several kilometers away, over rocky ground, but my hard-callused feet took me there in no time. The cave was another of mother's discoveries. She loved to explore. She loved to paint. She loved most things that challenged His will.

Most people stay in Camp. They don't want to explore. It frightens them. They are content to stay and work and go to Sermon. Go to Prayer. Content to do His will.

I never ask Choi to come with me. I won't risk that. I like Choi. I like his family. But I don't want to be a burden. I can care for myself. And what would Choi say? Would he tell the Community?

Mother once said, "Be careful, Grace. Please. They don't understand. They don't *want* to understand. For them, it is easier this way. The past was a mistake. It didn't work. They are deaf, dumb, and blind. They are scared. They see no beauty."

I wonder if Choi would see the beauty.

The cave is hidden in the side of a small rocky outcropping, tucked behind brambles and thorny bushes. Mother was right; this really is a place of stones and thorns. Pushing past the bushes, I step up, into the cave. The Community doesn't know about the cave. Mother got careless. They found her by the stream, using river mud and moistened flower petals as pigment, painting on an old, coarse piece of muslin. She wanted to be outside, I know, painting what she could see. I will not be as careless. Everything I need is in my head, in my mind.

The cave is cool and dim, but faint light leaks in from the

outside. It takes only a few moments for my eyes to adjust. I walk to the rear of the cave, sit down, and open one of father's books. I try to read, but some of the words are difficult. So I stand, go over to the rough cave wall. The dim light affords a murky view, but it is enough to see the paintings on the walls. Mother's paintings. They are beautiful. Most are simple scenes of nature: a sun-filled meadow, a dark forest, a mountain stream. Other's show pictures of the past, images I've glimpsed in father's books: strange structures both tall and squat. "Buildings," father said. "Houses. Like our tents, only permanent." And odd horseless carts that he called "cars." Images I wasn't supposed to know about. Things I wasn't supposed to see. Forbidden. According to His will.

I fish the apple skin from my pocket. I lick the skin, as mother taught me, and fold it. I press it lightly against the cave wall and gently brush the wet skin along the rough surface. It takes quite a few strokes, and I have to keep licking the skin, but soon I have a crude outline. One day, my art, my beauty, will grace these walls. And someone will find my beauty, and look at look at it and think and wonder.

Satisfied for the day, I sit down and look at my work. I smile. Then, remembering the mitten, I pull it from a pocket. I rub it against my face. It feels nice.

Standing, I make my way to the cave entrance and peer out. I must be careful. I don't want to end up like father. Or mother. At least not yet.

I picture mother on the cross on the high hill. Her eyes search me out. They are bright, vibrant, proud. She smiles at me. They place a crown of a thousand thorns on her head. Ling Chi, I think. She bleeds. And she bleeds.

We Pray.

It takes several days for her to bleed out, and I am there with her, Praying, the whole time. Just as I was for father. And, like father, when she finally bleeds out, I witness her eyes roll heavenwards in transcendent bliss.

It is His will.

WARM WET CIRCLES

Looking up from my desk, from the blinking green letters of the computer terminal, I watched the smoke-colored fog roll in and choke the building like a thick wool blanket. I gulped down the remaining tepid coffee from a Styrofoam cup, tossed the cup at a wire basket, but missed. There was a ring of condensation where the cup had sat. I poked curiously at it with a finger. The cheap veneer was still warm from the coffee. And it occurred to me, glancing around at my sullen co-workers with their disingenuous smiles, that they all wore a cheap veneer over their flesh and blood.

Bending to retrieve the wayward cup, my arm caught the tip of the keyboard tray and left a hunk of skin dangling from the corner. There was no blood. No pain. Indeed, there was only a minor scratch on my arm. But that strip of skin, that tiny piece of me, turned slowly in some phantom current, as if doing some delicate dance.

I peered out the window. The fog pressed ever closer.

I felt as if I were suffocating, so I went downstairs and around to the back alley for a quick toot of coke. That's where I found the dead man.

It was cool and misty, the air filled with a drear dampness. Downtown buildings stretched skyward, disappeared into ashen fog and dense smog. Gray. Always grey. And cold. A bit of nose candy was in order.

At first, I thought the dead man was just asleep. Just another drunk vagrant passed out in a downtown alleyway, blissfully unaware of anything but his own insular world. So I did a couple quick toots to clear my head, leaned back against the rough brick wall, and closed my eyes, waiting for the buzz. Once the edge was off, I opened my eyes and turned to head back to the office and the wonderfully exciting world of information technology. Back to the grey office with grey, unsmiling people. Back to lose another piece of myself to the corporate grind.

But the sleeping/dead man caught my eye. Something about the way he lay—face-down, stretched across the cement—seemed odd, unnatural; even for booze-laden homeless people.

So I sauntered down the alley, shoulders hunched, hands shoved deep in my pockets, trying for a casual, cool, nonchalant look, knowing I wasn't quite pulling it off, wondering why I cared to look cool, casual or nonchalant at all.

I gave the bloke a nudge with a booted foot. Nothing. I shivered, unsure whether it was from the cold or the coke. "Hey," I said, prodding him some more. "Hey. Get up." Still nothing. I squatted, leaned down for a look . . . and jumped back.

One great, blood-shot eye stared back at me. It didn't blink, didn't move, just stared. Steeling myself, I leaned in. That's when I noticed the rank smell of shit and urine, sweat and decay. It came off him in waves. Bile rose in my throat and I choked it down. He was obviously dead. Had been for some time. His clothes were a rumpled, uniform grey-brown. So was his hair. He lay splayed on the cold road, his fingers hooked claw-like as if he'd tried to crawl away from something, or tried to gain purchase from something that threatened to drag him away. That one staring eye looked at me reproachfully. The other half of his face lay hidden against the hard ground.

I'd never seen a real honest-to-goodness in-the-flesh dead person before.

Further down the alley something rattled, perhaps a garbage can. A plastic grocery bag appeared out of the fog, scuttled across the laneway, caught on my leg and wouldn't let go. I snatched at it, shoved it into a pocket.

Shit, I thought. What should I do? Ideally, I should have called someone. But I didn't. I felt a strange detachment. After all, it wasn't my bloody problem. Someone else would come along shortly and find him. Wouldn't they? Let them deal with it. I had things to do. I didn't know the chap.

Or did I? What if it was someone from the office? A co-worker or an acquaintance?

I chuckled at the absurdity. But to ease my troubled thoughts I reached down to turn him over and get a better look. At first, he wouldn't flip. I knelt down, grabbed hold of his greasy shirt and tugged. Slowly, he began to lift from the ground. But I saw the problem. It was his face, specifically the side that had been pressed to the cement. It was stuck. And as I pulled I saw his flesh string out like warm bubble gum that'd been trod upon, the way thin pink strands stretch between shoe and cement. Except this wasn't bubble gum, it was sallow yellow-grey skin with bits of dried blood, stretching, pulling.

Finally, with a wet snapping sound, I managed to yank the bloke free.

The wind moaned, but for a brief giddy moment I thought it was the dead man. Time to quit the nose candy.

Staring down at the dead man, I had to shake my head. If this was someone I knew I didn't know how I was going to identify him. The skin had ripped off one whole side of his face. What a fucking mess. And...

...I was eight-years-old again, watching the puppy chase the ball into the road, hearing the squeal of tires, the tiny yelp of fear, and a soft thud. I stood, watched the driver get out, place a hand on the broken dog. Watched the tail wag once, the body twitch. Then mom was there, grabbing my shoulders, ushering me into the house. And I didn't cry, didn't talk about it. The next morning I went out to the road. All that was left was a little blood and bone and fur. Then the rain came, washing away the remnants, and that's when I cried.

I trembled, wished I had another line of coke.

Breaking from my reverie I noticed the skein of flesh stuck to the cement, how the taffy-pulled quality of it wavered, as if beckoning. A queer feeling came over me. Remembering the plastic bag in my trousers, I fished it out and, minding that no one was watching, used it as a glove. With a bit of effort I plucked the skin from the ground, turning the bag inside out so as to trap the tissue inside.

With one last look at the deceased, I stepped over his body and hurried back to the office with my prize clutched tightly in hand.

Curiously, the strip of skin on the keyboard tray was gone. Disappeared.

As was the case lately, I couldn't work, couldn't concentrate. I'd stare out the grimy window, at the sooty haze that choked the office tower like a great grey hand, my thoughts jumbled, foggy like the outside world. Far below me, in that foggy outside world, a dead man lay in an alley. I had a piece of him in a drawer in my desk. A macabre memento.

Later, when I got home, I placed the dead man's flesh in an old, unused cigar box.

It didn't bother me at all that I had the skin of a dead man in a humidor in a dark closet in my apartment. There was something uniquely intimate about it that spoke to my peculiar sensibilities. A fragment; a puzzle; a thin, torn, membranous memory.

CR80

The following morning, before going up to the office, I stole a peek down the alleyway. Seeing nothing untoward, I strolled down the alley, whistling. The dead man, as I suspected, was gone. There were curious brownish stains on the ground; ring-shaped, like moist, puckered lips. Otherwise, there was no other sign to tell me that a dead man lay here yesterday.

In a city this size there must be hundreds, perhaps thousands, of homeless. Where do they go? What happens to them when they die? Do municipal workers come by in big yellow trucks to scoop them up like road kill? They can't just disappear.

The rest of the day (indeed, the rest of the week) was uneventful. I managed to perform even the most perfunctory of tasks without the benefit of any illegal stimulant. Wonders.

Then, early Saturday morning on my way home from the news stand (where I picked up The Guardian and some Dentyne) I saw another dead man.

He was in a small side alley off the main street. It was still grey and dull and chill, a faint mist hanging in the air. The cold seeped into my bones. Christ, where was the fucking sun?

As I passed the tiny side street, I briefly glimpsed a dark huddled mass in the periphery of my vision. It was still early enough that the streets were relatively empty, so I wandered down to the crumpled bundle of rags.

Indeed, it was another dead homeless man. Were there no homeless women? I wondered.

The man lay on his side, his sleeveless right arm tucked under his head as if asleep. Except he wasn't going to wake. This was the long big sleep.

So I rolled him over onto his back. His arm gave some resistance, but pulled free, leaving clumps of grey-green skin on the ground. I didn't recognize him. He resembled the other dead man; bearded, greasy, unkempt.

Odd that life should be categorized and stereotyped. All the homeless looked the same. All my grey and brown-suited co-workers resembled each other. What about me? Where did I fit?

His eyes were wide open, and a small Mona Lisa smile creased his face. My eyes were drawn to the patches of flesh—the pieces of him—that clung to the pavement. What a strange amalgam: flesh and stone.

Bending, I tried to grab hold of a piece of fleshy tissue, but it was too short, too ingrained in the cement, and I could gain no purchase. I grabbed a piece of cardboard that lay nearby and with shoveling and scraping motions managed to peel the majority of the flesh from the ground. Carefully, I placed the fleshy fragments into the bag alongside the newspaper.

When I got back to the apartment, I placed the skin in the humidor alongside the earlier remnants. Whereas the two dead men had seemed so similar, their skin, their remains, were completely different. One was thin and tissue-like, the other a mix of small flakes and hardened little nubs. The irony wasn't lost on me. I wondered what the vestiges of me would look like.

The following day, Sunday, on my way back to the news stand to buy Dentyne (one can never have enough chewing gum) I took a quick detour down the side street where I'd found my second dead man.

Gone. Nothing left but small, dark, circular stains that glistened suggestively. I bent, stroked the dark marks. They were moist... and warm. I was mildly aroused.

I went home, read the paper, chewed gum and drank tea. I tried not to notice the fog outside my window, thick and oppressive, pressing in all around me. Eventually, I closed the blinds and took to bed.

୧୫ଚ

Days passed, one like the other, grey and unending. I withdrew from the small circle of friends (if you could call them that) and acquaintances that made up my world. They were cool and aloof. Or perhaps I was. Surprisingly, I stayed away from the Cocaine.

One particularly dismal and rainy Tuesday I stopped in at a local pub. It was quiet, mostly empty, and the gloom outside pervaded the dark, smoky room. I was cold. Cold and alone.

I sat down at the bar, ordered a pint of the local brew. Sipping the bland ale I noticed several rings of moisture atop the honey-colored wood. Remnants of the lives of ordinary people. Passing my hand through the residue, I wasn't surprised to find that they were warm wet circles. I imagined them opening and closing like hungry little mouths. I imagined my penis in just such a mouth.

Later that evening, alone in my room, I took out the humidor, stared at the dead skin, rubbed my fingers over the texture. A pleasant quiver shook me.

I'd never been good with intimacy.

୧୫ଚ

Early the following day I called work, told them I was sick and wouldn't be in. I tried to alter my voice, give it a cough-like quality, but didn't convince even myself. They wouldn't miss me anyway.

I didn't shower or shave. I skipped breakfast. I slipped on a windbreaker and wandered out into the streets. I headed downtown. It didn't bother me that I might pass by the office. I didn't fucking care. I just walked and walked. And as I walked the air became dense, moist, cloudy. The constant damp chill soaked into me, and I hugged myself for warmth. I passed people who seemed to be streaming by in a rush; all dressed in browns and greys the colour of moths and rocks, gaping at me, their faces distorted. It was as if I was moving in slow motion. The fog got thicker. The streams of people dissipated. The streets became unfamiliar. I walked and walked, and it seemed that all the streets were alike, that I'd walked this same stretch over and over, twisting and turning through dark back alleys, wading through gasoline-choked puddles that glimmered with a strange fish-like iridescence. And I was reminded of little fish mouths gasping for air. Reminded of odd dark stains and warm wet circles.

Finally, I found him in a greasy cardboard lean-to in an anonymous back alley. He lay face-down, arms stretched wide, palms pressed to the ground as if he'd just done a set of pushups and needed a rest. Smiling, I grabbed hold of one hand and tugged. It was spongy and gummy, but pulled free without much effort. I fished the sandwich bag from my pocket (the type that zips neatly shut) and scraped the decaying flesh from the ground, scooping it into the waiting bag. The skin was wet and smelled faintly of smoke or ash. I zipped the bag closed and made my way back to the apartment, making a mental note of the main intersection closest to this side alleyway. Once safely home, out of the grey fog, I deposited the new flesh into the humidor. The moist, rank skin contrasted nicely with my other pieces.

Satisfied, I fell into bed with my clothes on. Just before succumbing to slumber I recalled I hadn't eaten anything all day. I wasn't hungry.

And when I woke bright and early the next day, I still wasn't hungry.

I left the apartment immediately, not bothering to call in to work though it was only mid-week. Chances are they wouldn't even miss me. In a city this size people go missing every day. I wore the same clothes as the day before, and I still hadn't shaved or brushed my teeth. It was damp outside, the air heavy, seemingly thrumming with queer electricity.

The alley wasn't hard to locate once I found the intersection. I hurried down it, searching for my dead man though I knew he'd be gone. There was no sign of him. The rain had destroyed the cardboard lean-to, rendering it a sodden mess. I got down on my hands and knees, brushed away the detritus of cardboard, dirt and old newspaper. There, on the wet cement, hundreds of round circles—like suckers from an octopus—pulsed and writhed. I smiled. I was ready.

Pressing my face to the pavement, I lay down on the warm wet circles.

I always wondered what happened to homeless people. They just seem to vanish. Yet, if you look hard enough, you can find remnants of them.

I wondered if I would disappear without a trace.

PAPER THIN

A fat black fly landed on the kitchen table, beside her cereal bowl. She brought her hand down, squashing the fly. It left a thin smear of pinkish blood.

Miriam hadn't noticed how thin, how transparent, the world had become until after her split with Alan. It was as if nothing was real. Everything a façade.

And that's what her time with Alan had turned out to be; a lie.

Of course, she'd spent the last six years of her life with Alan, planning, dreaming, loving. She hadn't been paying much attention to anything else. Nothing else had mattered.

Until now.

She found an apartment, on the east side, far enough away that she doubted she'd run into *him*. Besides, she knew all his haunts. Knew what places to avoid. And it wasn't likely he'd venture this way. People were leaving the east side in droves. Shops were closing. Garbage and stray dogs filled the streets. And people of questionable character took residence in abandoned buildings and businesses. Miriam hadn't wanted to live so close to the squatters, but it was all she could afford. Soon enough, she thought, when some time had passed, she'd move back to the city proper or to a quiet suburb.

Six years and she was on her own again. Wasted years, she now knew. Six years of building a life that never materialized. A life that never happened. Looking around her Spartan apartment – an apartment meant for one, not two, or, God forbid, a family—Miriam wondered how many other lives never happened.

How much of it was real?

Miriam first began wondering about her reality when the letter arrived. It was from Alan. He'd somehow managed to track down her new address. That frightened her a little bit. And angered her, as well. She tore open the envelope, unfolded the thin, tissue-like parchment. The letter was written in Alan's unfailingly perfect script. At first, everything about Alan had seemed perfect. Shaking, Miriam read the letter as angry tears welled in her eyes. Alan was so sorry. He took blame for everything. (As if he could). He wished her a happy life. Miriam blinked, rubbed her eyes. The words ran and blurred. Drying her eyes, she went to the window, held the letter up to the meager light that shone in, tried to decipher the ink that ran like thin black blood. She thought she saw other words trapped in the parchment, under the outer layer. Words like "slut", "bitch", and "ball-buster". She dropped the letter then, watched it float to the floor like a ruined sparrow. She pulled the window blind, but it was thin, too thin, and a dingy haze seeped in.

Truly alone now for the first time in her life, Miriam began to see things in a different light. After all, with her parents dead, there was nobody else she was beholden to. Whereas before, with Alan, life seemed predictably pleasant and routine, she now noticed things she hadn't before. She *saw* things. Things that hid beneath, between, and behind the thinly-veiled world she'd never known existed. It was all a new world to her. And she couldn't quite determine if that pleased her or not.

This morning she felt like going to the market. Miriam had taken some time off work, and was finding it difficult to fill her days. After a light breakfast, and a failed attempt to clean the smeared fly from the table, she climbed on board bus 102 and headed toward Front Street and the market. It was on the eastern border of the city, not an area Alan ever had reason to frequent, so she felt no great fear in venturing out that way. She took a seat in the back of the bus, her thoughts drifting to the low rumble of the bus engine as it bounced along the narrow streets. The windows were caked in dirt and soot. She wiped her sleeve across the pane, but it just left a greasy smudge. Peering through the dirt, Miriam saw endless piles of refuse; broken windows in shops; forlorn homes; smashed and twisted bicycles. The streets glistened, as if covered in gelatin.

Shabby vagrants ducked down side alleys as the bus approached. Dogs roamed freely. Large birds circled in the grey sky, occasionally swooping in on a pile of garbage and flying away with something thin and red dangling from their beaks. The sky itself seemed to waver, like a curtain in a breeze, and Miriam briefly wondered what was behind the thin curtain. What would she see if she were able to reach up and pull back the covering? Sighing, Miriam turned from the window. The bus was empty save for her and the round, pink driver. No one else got on. Indeed, the bus didn't once stop until Miriam stood and pulled the cord to indicate she wanted off. The driver squealed to a sudden halt and shot Miriam a feral look. It wasn't even a proper stop, but the rear doors opened and Miriam hurried down the steps before they closed on her. She had a feeling she'd be trapped in the bus forever if she didn't get out, endlessly bumping down dark, grease-laden streets as black birds circled in a darkening sky.

Miriam walked the short distance to the market. Few people were about. Due, she suspected, to the fact that it was grey and sullen, and only midweek. A young mother strolled by, pushing a carriage. She remembered that they'd wanted to have children, Alan and her. Together.

Bored sellers stood behind counters in weather-beaten stalls. Miriam passed people hawking fruits and vegetables, flowers, fish, eggs and poultry, and other sundry materials. She hadn't come for any particular item, so she browsed slowly, wondering if she should bother with anything at all. Eventually, though, she purchased some loose tea, some peppers, and farm fresh eggs. She'd never seen eggs so large. She'd make herself an omelet for supper.

Stopping at a newsstand, Miriam stared at all the magazines and newspapers. She reached out, touched the newsprint, marveled at how thin it was. She rubbed the page between thumb and forefinger, smudging a bold headline, leaving a greyish ash-like stain on her fingertips. The headline, much like Alan, glared like an accusation.

Miriam turned, headed for home, not chancing another bus ride. Besides, it was still early. It wouldn't be dark for hours. The walk would do her good.

Once she was out of the market, the streets quickly became deserted.

Barren.

It was, Miriam thought, an altogether detestable word.

She walked westward under a great grey sky flecked with winged things. The street still glistened suggestively. A damp smell of rot and mold wafted in the air. The sidewalk was a cracked and broken path, heaving up from the earth. Nothing walked the street with her; no cats, no dogs, no men, no women, and no children. Especially no children.

Clutching her small bag from the market, Miriam quickened her pace. She passed by several small houses with square windows like eyes. But the all the blinds were drawn, giving the impression of sleep or rest. And sometimes she thought she saw things behind those thin eyelids. Things that flitted and fluttered, scuttled and crawled. So she put her head down and hurried along the heaving sidewalk.

Until she came across the small pink thing.

Miriam stopped, her heart racing. *Surely, it couldn't be,* she thought. And stooping to inspect it further she found it was a bird, just a tiny little bird, possibly a scant few hours old. The bird was pink and hairless, lying on the cracked sidewalk. Miriam stared at it. She could see through its skin—its thin, thin skin – into its fragile little body. She saw tiny, delicate bones. She saw round little eyes under thin pink lids.

Then the bird opened its mouth and Miriam gasped.

She quickly scooped the bird up. Miriam gently stroked its head with a finger and the bird opened its eyes. Cradling the bird in the palm of her free hand, Miriam rushed home, unmindful of anything but a stark singular purpose: *Save the baby bird. Save the baby... bird?*

In the apartment, Miriam dropped the bag and raced to the linen closet. She reached in, grabbed a large fluffy towel. Back in the living room, she placed the towel on the loveseat (and the irony wasn't lost on her), and formed it into a rudimentary nest-like object. With great care, Miriam laid the tiny creature in the towel, pushing in the sides a bit to try and keep the bird warm. An eye winked once, slowly, and a wing fluttered, once.

She moved to the kitchen. She noticed a faint pinkish mark on the kitchen table. It occurred to her that she should feed the bird, but hadn't a clue as to what. Miriam decided on warm milk, the old standby. As the milk warmed in a pot on the burner, she rummaged around in a drawer for an eye-dropper. Finding one, she rinsed it off, drew some milk into it, and went to fetch the bird.

But the bird was dead.

The bird didn't stir. Miriam nudged it with a finger. It was cold, unresponsive. She waited, waited, waited… Nothing.

Sighing, Miriam folded the towel around the dead creature. She went back to the kitchen and placed the bundle into the trash.

She'd tried. Hadn't Alan seen that she'd tried?

Miriam went to the window to catch a breath of fresh air. The blind was still drawn. As she moved to draw the blind up, movement caught her eye. The thin blind wavered, pulsed, as if alive, as if something lived, trapped, behind the thin membrane. She stepped back. Blinked. The blind was flat and smooth and still. Miriam pulled down and the blind shot up. It was almost dark outside. Twilight encased the world in a luminous grey cloak. A paper thin veil that failed to conceal the black things that circled and swirled and swooped without end in the pearl and pewter sky.

Raising the window, Miriam ducked her head out and breathed deeply. The heavy air stank of sour milk and week-old fish. Something or someone cried out in the black night. She closed the window, retreated into the main room to retrieve her grocery bag.

Back in the kitchen, she opened her small refrigerator and began to put away the peppers and eggs she'd purchased. The eggs were large, the size of tennis balls, but relatively light in weight. Miriam held one up to the light. The shell was thin. She felt it would crack if she gripped it too tightly. For a moment, the egg appeared to pulse like the window blind had. And Miriam imagined she saw something in the egg. Something small and growing.

89

Then, before she could prevent it, the egg slipped from Miriam's hand and smashed on the floor. Startled, she knelt and inspected the mess. The yolk had split and ran. The white of the egg reminded her of the greasy streets. But there wasn't anything else in the egg. It had just been an ordinary egg, after all. Miriam scooped the gooey mess into the trashcan.

With her appetite gone, Miriam made some tea and sat down on the loveseat. She sipped carefully at the hot liquid. The tea was weak, insipid, the colour of thin blood and smeared flies. The window blind quivered. Dark shapes stirred behind the veil. From the hallway, something wailed. A child, perhaps. Her eye was drawn to the long pink smear on the kitchen table.

For many hours Miriam sat in the small room, among the gathering gloom, cradling her cold empty cup. She dozed. She dreamt unpleasant dreams. The sound of the postman startled her awake.

Miriam stood groggily and went to the door. She stooped and picked up the mail where it had landed on the mat; promotional flyers, a water bill, and a letter.

From Alan.

She tore open the envelope, read it, and let it drop to ground. Numbly, Miriam went to the kitchen to grab a bite to eat. She grabbed a bowl, and an egg from the refrigerator. And when she cracked the egg and nothing came out, she wasn't the least bit surprised.

Instead, Miriam fixed herself a bowl of cereal.

A fat black fly landed on the kitchen table, beside her cereal bowl. She brought her hand down, squashing the fly.

It left a thin smear of pinkish blood.

METASTASIS

The car radio was on. Del Shannon was singing.

Run run run runaway.

If you were to stop him (and that was unlikely, given the fact he only stopped for food and gas and bathroom breaks) and ask him where he was headed, he'd blink, maybe smile, chew harder on the ever present toothpick sticking from his mouth and shrug his shoulders.

Fact was, Terence didn't know where he was going. Hadn't known at any point in his life where he was headed. Not through grade school, high school, college, a loveless, childless, miserably failed marriage had he at any point known where he was going, or where he'd end up.

Funny that the realization took so long to sink in.

And now, here he was in the twilight of his life, driving a straight, lonely prairie highway in a six-year old Buick, the windows down, the wind whipping what little hair he had left, the sun shining as he rocketed past field after field of golden grass swaying in the summer breeze. Grass that waved and whispered hypnotically.

And still Terence had no destination in mind. It was enough that he was driving, going forward, moving along the prairies as if—like the sun and the clouds, the wind and the grass, the dark ribbon of highway—he was part of the land's fabric. Inexorable, like the changing seasons.

When he was young his dad often took him on long Sunday drives in the country. He hadn't especially liked it, but it made his father happy. His father would smile, look over at him, point out odd clouds or interesting trees, comment on the weather or the Red Sox, his hand tapping on the steering wheel as Del Shannon and Roy Orbison crooned from the radio.

"Isn't this fun?" his father would ask.

He'd feign a smile, shrug his shoulders. "Yep."

"Damn right, son." And he'd open the glove box, carefully steering with one hand, reach in and pull out a small wax envelope. He'd thumb open the envelope, hold it out for him. "Go ahead, boy. Take one."

So he would grab one of the cinnamon-flavored toothpicks and stick it in his mouth. He didn't really like the things—too hot—but it humored his old man. And sometimes they would pull over, jump out of the car and run, laughing, through the high grass of a meadow. Later they would stop for a couple of bottles of cold Lime Rickey. That, to Terence, was the best part of the best day of the week. Because come Monday he had school and homework and chores. Responsibilities. Responsibilities were for grownups. Why was everyone in such a hurry to grow up? Even as a child, one who'd at that point never experienced the bitter tang of love, he'd promised himself that if he should ever have children he'd let them live and laugh and play as long as they liked. Let them love. Why should he hurry them to grow up and be all serious?

But Terence never had children.

He smiled, rolling the toothpick around his mouth. It was a plain old toothpick. You couldn't find the flavored ones around anymore. He wondered if you could still buy Lime Rickey. Probably not, he mused. Some things, unfortunately, do change.

The times they are a-changing.

Dylan. One of his dad's favorites.

His dad was long dead.

It was mid-morning and hot. The lemon-yellow sun blazed in a high bright blue sky. Terence pressed down on the accelerator. The road was wide and clear and stretched for as far as his eyes could see. It seemed to go on forever. He hadn't passed any gas stations or rest stops all day. The smooth black asphalt rolled under his car like some unending roll of carpet. He drove on, past field after field of tall straw grass waving languidly in the slight breeze. It reminded him of those nature and adventure shows he'd watch as a kid, where they'd dive into some dark part of the ocean to investigate its mysteries, and bright antenna and feelers would wave and flutter on screen like strange spindly fingers beckoning. Is that what the grass was telling him? Was it waving to him? Beckoning?

Mutual of Omaha's Wild Kingdom.

That was one of the shows he and his father would watch together. They always timed their Sunday drives to get home in time for Marlin Perkins. And they would sit silently on the couch together, watching events unfold on the Serengeti or the Great Plains.

Terence looked up into the bright glare of the sun, blinked. He pulled at the collar of his sweat-stained shirt. How he wished for a convertible. An old Ford, the size of a boat, one you could really settle into. A cruising car. Or a Mustang. Damn! He'd always wanted a Mustang. He smiled. A young man's car. Now he had a Buick. An old man's car. The smile faltered on his lips. He didn't know how or when it happened, but suddenly he was an old man. An old man and his Buick. Nothing too romantic about that. Not like a boy and his dog.

His dog. Rex. Long dead.

Just about everyone and everything he once cherished was long dead.

Everybody dies. We die a little every day, Terence thought. All of us are dying.

Even me.

There was something up ahead. It was a small wooden stand by the side of the road, the kind you'd see in the country, selling corn and fruit and pies. Terence slowed, turned off the radio, brought the big Buick to a halt several yards from the stand. He stepped out of the car, spit out the toothpick, rubbed a tired hand on the back of his tired neck, and sauntered over to the stand.

"Howdy," Terence said to the man behind the makeshift counter.

The man was big, barrel-shaped, with thick fingers drumming the wooden counter top. His eyes were bright. There was something vaguely familiar about the man but Terence couldn't quite place it. The man smiled, revealing broken yellow teeth.

"Howdy, yourself," the man said, beaming.

Terence glanced about. There were no pies, no peaches, no husked corn or apples. No produce of any kind.

"Who are you?" Terence asked.

"A friend," said the smiling man. "Everyone needs a friend. Especially out here."

A small folded booklet lay on the counter. The man picked up the booklet, shoved it at Terence.

"There you go," the man said, idly scratching the side of his nose. "Lucky you. That's the last one."

"The last one?" Terence said.

The man shrugged. "Yep. Been a busy day."

Terence looked up and down the desolate highway, back to the man. "A busy day?"

The man nodded.

Terence studied the booklet, unfolded it. It was a map. He wagged it at the man. "What's this for?"

"Well, in case you get lost, of course."

"Yes, of course," Terence said, turning the map over in his hands. "How silly of me."

The man looked skyward, frowned, turned to Terence. "Best get going, there's a storm a-coming."

Terence scrutinized the sky. It was clear and cloudless. "I see. But I don't know where I'm going. I don't know where the road leads."

The man winked. "I think you do. It runs straight and true. Now run along."

"But. . . ."

"Hurry," the man said. "And promise me you'll not look back."

"Not look back?" Terence said.

"Right. There's no going back."

"Okay."

The man waved an impatient hand.

So Terence trudged back and climbed into the car. He placed the map on the passenger seat, idly noting the long continuous road marked in red that cut straight through the land. He steered the car onto the road and eased it past the roadside stand.

Terence glanced to the side. The man was still smiling. He waved at Terence. A slight breeze whooshed through the air. The high grass swished. "Good luck, son," said the man or the grass or the wind.

Terence turned, half-smiling, and stared at the road ahead. Clouds rolled in, clotting the graying sky.

There's a storm a-coming.

Terence hoped there wasn't a storm coming. He'd weathered enough of them in his life so far. But life was a sad sequence of storms and tranquility, shadow and light. The key was to keep moving, stay the course, and never look back.

Stay the course. That's something his father would have said. Was he in danger of becoming his father? A metastasis? Or was it too late for that?

Fat drops of rain fell, plinked off the hood. Terence rolled up the window.

The times they are a-changing.

Plink. Plink-plink.

Terence liked the rain. It was steady, unchanging, comforting.

He switched on the windshield wipers. They flapped intermittently, *phulap, phulap,* like leathery crow wings. He leaned forward to peer through the blurry windshield. Movement up ahead caught his eye and Terence slowed, brought the car to a halt in the middle of the slick road. A yellow raincoat shape approached, opened the side door and stuck a hooded head into the car.

Terence stared.

"Are you going to invite me in?" she asked. "It's getting cold you know. There's a storm coming."

Terence frowned. "I know. Get in."

"Thanks." She climbed in, sat on the map, removed her hood, shook her hair. Terence was reminded of a dog shaking water from its coat.

Rex. His boyhood dog.

Terence pulled away, stared straight ahead. "How far you going?" he asked, eyes on the black road.

95

She chuckled. He could feel her gaze on him. Silence, then, "Not as far as you. Not yet."

They rode a while in silence, Terence watching the road and the grass in the steady drizzle. She fidgeted, her hands twisting in her lap.

The road ran on, straight, unwavering. The tires hissed wetly on the smooth, slippery pavement. The rain fell. Plink. Plink. The wipers wiped. Phulap. Phulap. His heart beat. Boom. Boom.

She coughed, reached a hand over and placed it gently on his arm. "What did he say?"

Terence chanced a look, saw the wide liquid eyes and his heart hurt, bled a little more. "Who?" he asked.

She turned, looked back down the receding road. "*Him.*"

"Oh." He snorted, gripped the wheel tightly, knuckles whitening. "Is that what this is about?"

"N-no, I just thought. . . ." She pulled her hand away. "Never mind."

"He wished me luck."

Good luck, son.

"Oh," she said.

"What about you?" Terence asked. "Did you see him too? Did he give you a map?"

"No. No map for me." She looked away. "I think I'll get out here. This is far enough."

"If you're sure."

"Yes."

"It's raining. You'll be cold and wet."

She pulled the hood up over her head. "Someone else will come by."

Yes, Terence thought, someone else. Of course. She'd found someone else.

Terence pulled over. She scrambled out of the car, stood with the door open, staring in, rain dripping from her slicker.

That's when he noticed the swell in her belly. "You're pregnant," Terence said.

She touched her stomach. "I always wanted children. It was no secret."

96

Terence tried a smile, but failed. "I understand."

"I'm sorry," she said, then closed the door.

Terence drove off. "Me too," he whispered, not looking back. "Me too."

Back on the road, the raining sky above, the wet champagne-colored grass on the sides, the ground beneath his feet. It was like some long unending tunnel, and Terence felt a little claustrophobic, as if they were all pressing in on him, closing in on him, and there was nowhere to go, nowhere to escape.

He reached over, plucked the map from where she'd sat on it. It was damp and soft. The red-marked road bled east to west. *Metastasis*.

Terence was heading west. Bleeding west. Go west young man.

BOOM! Just thunder. Not his bleeding, broken heart. In the distance lightning slashed across the slate sky. Terence twisted the knob for the radio. Del Shannon was singing about a little runaway, walking along, wondering what went wrong with a love so strong. He grinned. Funny how he even liked the old man's music now.

The miles passed. The rain continued. The sky went from slate to shiny soot. He tapped his hand on the steering wheel in time with the music.

There was something in the road. A small dark shape. Terence slammed the brakes and the car screeched to a sideways halt several feet in front of the dim form. He stepped out of the car, stuttered forward then stopped, staring.

It was a dog. It stood in the rain, tail wagging.

Terence bent, held out a hand, ignoring the pelting rain. "Here, boy, here," he beckoned. The dog yelped, its tail whipping.

"Come, boy, come."

The dog yelped once more then bounded off into the high border grass, disappearing.

Terence scratched his head, thought momentarily about going after the creature. It wanted to play, he knew. Dogs loved to play. Rex had loved to play. But Terence thought he should keep moving, keep going forward, so he shuffled back into the car and continued on his way, down the dark prairie highway, the radio singing run run run runaway.

Terence blinked. He imagined he saw two small children, a boy and a girl, at the side of the road. The girl clutched a teddy bear and a pink umbrella. The boy had a Red Sox cap and a ball glove. Moisture filled Terence's eyes. He blinked again and the children were gone. Well, not exactly gone, Terence mused, they never existed. Not in his real life.

No children.

He sighed, pressed on in the deepening gloom, letting the road take him to its end. It wouldn't be long now, he thought.

And he was right. The road ended. Terence brought the Buick to an abrupt stop. He left the engine running, got out of the car, and ambled to the road's end. High yellow grass fluttered and danced in the wind and rain. Terence gazed around. The grass was to his left, his right, and in front of him, waving hypnotically. He didn't turn around because he'd promised himself he wasn't looking back.

What was he to do?

But he knew, of course. It was the only logical thing for him to do. He'd continue on his journey. There was no looking back.

So he stepped into the grass.

He was young again, a child, happy and carefree, racing through the tall grass, chasing his father in the golden meadow maze. Nearby, a dog barked. A small joyous yelp, as if it had just gotten a bone. Rex? And Terence pushed on, in the twilight, through the unending fields that stretched all around him, from horizon to horizon, unending. Unchanging.

Terence ran, searching through the grassland. "Rex? Dad?"

He ran, searched, pushed through deep wet grass that slapped his face.

"Dad? Dad?"

Cool peppermint rain fell from the sky. The honey grass swayed and sang, and to Terence it was Del Shannon singing about a little runaway walking in the rain.

It grew dark. Terence began to cry. The grass sighed and moaned. The wind sang.

I'm walking in the rain, tears are falling and I feel the pain.

He hurried forward, lost.

SUMMER GHOSTS

It is a ghost town.

At the crest of the street I stop, catch my breath. The air is thick and yellow and hazy. Sour lemonade sky. A hacking wheeze wracks my chest. *One more*, I think. One more coughing fit and these old bones will shatter. Like the deserted town, I'm a ghost of my former self.

The town crouches under a sallow sky. The street is desolate, of course, and mostly quiet. I can't hear a thing except faint whispers on a sour breeze. Shuttered, abandoned houses sag under the weight of years of neglect. Skeletal, withered trees dot the scrub grass on the boulevard. Broken glass and old tires litter the ruined road. The sidewalk is cracked, heaving up in places, as if the earth itself is trying to devour the town. I smell, faintly, a sour tang; a mix of cooked flesh and ammonia. Even after all these years the stench still lingers.

I see the house, our old house, a dirty grey thing, falling in on itself. Broken. At the end of the street, silent, sits the old black mill. Black and dead and forgotten. The black chimney juts into the sickly sky, its edges limned in yellow hoarfrost.

I gaze down the street and imagine an earlier time. I see a little blond dead boy, Joey Battaglia, smiling in perpetuity from a sepia portrait. I see a large pink hog, wide-eyed, snorting, running in fear. I see the black mill belching thick black smoke. I see a wispy black wraith, my father. And I see poor little Liam.

I see a mirror.

I see me.

I see a ghost.

CR80

It was the summer of ghosts.

My first ghost. My first real memory. Because that's all that memories are, really. Ghosts. And that's all that I have left to me. Memories and ghosts.

I was 12-years-old that summer, and I can't remember my life before that. It's like the first 11 years of my life were removed, like thin white chalk from a chalkboard, the eraser smudging the wavy lines into oblivion. Those first 11 years were a succession of moves from house to house, from school to school, as my parents lurched from job to job. It was a whirlwind time, and my young mind, instead of twisting the chalky lines, had simply erased them.

It was early summer. I'd just finished grade 7, and once the school year was over my parents packed everything up and drove us a couple hours east, to our new house. Liam, my younger brother, wailed the whole trip. His face was pink and pudgy, covered in snot and tears.

"Why do we have to move again?" I asked mom.

She gave me a withering look. "Your father has a new job. We found a nice place we can afford near his work. You'll like it."

We moved into a narrow two-storey Victorian on Cumberland St. When we pulled up in front of the house, a fat black bird eyed us from the top of a sickly tree. It squawked, flew off into a wedge of grey sky. At the far end of the street a wide black building with a tall black tower belched thick black smoke into a perpetually grey sky. The air on the street carried a faint yellowish hue. It was thick and still, and reminded me of dead, brittle cocoons. Ancient parchment. If I reached out, it'd probably shatter.

Our house was a sagging, molding, paint-peeling monstrosity that smelled like rotting wood and dead leaves. The house had a steep wooden staircase, with a wide ornate banister and thick wooden slats leading to the top floor. Adjacent to the stairway was a narrow hallway that lead to the kitchen and dining room. The wall opposite the staircase was stark and empty save for an oval mirror in a thick, dull, brassy frame.

That first day we moved in, the mirror was on the wall. The previous owner had left it, forgotten or unwanted. I remember stopping in the hallway, looking up, pointing, as mother and father scurried by with boxes of dishes and clothes and old ornaments. Mother stopped, holding a box labeled "Kitchen," a look of exasperation on her face. "It's just a mirror, Jerome. We'll keep it, if you like." We did keep it. But I didn't like it. Entering the cold house that first day, and seeing the large dark mirror on the wall, startled me. It reminded me of a large, cloudy eye.

And though the mirror filled me with a queer unease, it also piqued my interest. What was it doing there? Why was it left behind?

As a curious boy, standing in the hallway staring up at the mirror, I could barely see the top part of the milky glass reflecting the staircase behind me. And each time I looked up at the mirror, I imagined I saw movement in the dark glass, a languorous swirling of dark smoke, dark mystery. Of course, youthful trepidations aside, I had to see into the mirror. I had to find out what hid in its dark depths. Curiosity got the better of me.

Less than a week in our new house I climbed up the stairs to inspect the mirror. I turned, grinning unpleasantly, and peered at the dark oval. The mirror was old, patchy, smoke-coloured, as if the reflective parts had faded, leaving behind strange dark spots. The edges were fuzzy, distorted, wavy like a small-town funhouse mirror.

Leaning forward, resting my head against the thick wooden slats, I gazed into the mirror. I saw a small face . . . but it wasn't mine.

The round pale face gazed at me impassively, eyes unblinking. The reflective mirror edges pulled at the face like soft taffy. Who was it? It couldn't be me. Could it?

I gripped the wooden stair slats and strained forward, trying to make out the face. I pressed my face between the varnished rails and, suddenly, my head popped between the thin wooden planks and poked through to the other side of the banister. Somehow, I'd slipped my head between the gap. I looked into the mirror then, and saw that it was indeed my face staring back at me, because the

101

eyes were wide in surprise and the mouth was open in a startled "O."

Inching backward, I tried to pull my head through the railing. It wouldn't budge. My little heart pounded. My brother screamed. I tried again, gripping the rails tightly and pulling, my feet scrabbling for purchase on the slick stairs. But my ears would catch on the slats, preventing my head from slipping free.

I panicked. I struggled. I screamed. As I screamed, as I thrashed against the wooden slats, my mirror image smiled, slightly; a coy, mischievous grin that stopped me cold. And it wasn't me looking out from the silvered mirror. It was some other me.

Later, in my bed, after the firemen had come and cut me from the stairs, I wondered about the *real* me, not the mirror me. Because even at that age I knew the boy in the mirror wasn't real. He was some tiny ghost boy.

If the boy in the mirror wasn't real, was I real?

෬෫

Mrs. Battaglia was a fat old lady who wore pink and yellow sun dresses, and smelled like burnt garlic and oily fish. But she served me lemonade and sticky buns on her rickety front porch. I liked her. She owned the house next door, and was always out front tending to her little garden or sweeping her sidewalk.

All the houses on Cumberland Street were old and in disrepair. Cracked windows, splintered driveways, sagging gutters, leaning fences. The maples and oaks that lined the street were stunted, twisted with disease. A strange electric chemical smell, like burnt hair, tainted the yellow air. The mill, I presumed. But it wasn't the mill. It was the hogs.

There were no other children on Cumberland. Everyone was old, like Mrs. Battaglia.

We'd been in the new house less than a week, and Mrs. Battaglia had taken a shine to me. She liked to talk, and I liked to listen. My only friends that summer were Liam and Mrs. Battaglia.

102

Mrs. Battaglia lived alone. Mr. Battaglia, I learned, died some years earlier. "Sickness in the lungs," Mrs. Battaglia said, spooning sugar into her lemonade.

I took a bite from my sticky bun, slurped my drink. "Cancer?" I asked.

She blinked, paused, seemed to think about my question. She smiled wistfully, turned and gazed down the street. The sun sat behind the mill, its orangey light mixing with the black smoke to lend the sky a look of shimmering burnt copper.

Mrs. Battaglia leaned over, pinched my cheek. "No, no, Jerry. Not cancer. What do you know of such things?"

I shrugged. We sat silently, sipping our lemonades. I heard her spoon clink against the tall glass. The thick, slow, summer afternoon ticked on.

"Everybody dies, Jerry," Mrs. Battaglia finally said. "Everybody."

"What about children?" I asked.

She sighed. "Even children die."

I licked sticky icing from my fingers. She didn't understand so I asked her again. "Do you have any children?"

Mrs. Battaglia put her glass down, folded her hands in her lap, looked at me piteously. "Yes. Well, no, actually." She leaned forward, smiled, stroked my cheek this time instead of her usual pinch. "I'm sorry," she said. "I never know how to answer that question."

Her mood had changed, and it was my fault. I stood. "I have to go," I said, and scooted off the porch and sprinted home.

CR80

I stepped out the front door one afternoon into the pale grey-yellow air to find Liam on the cracked sidewalk playing with a dead thing. I thought it was a stuffed toy. As I approached I saw his little hands wrapped tight around a crow. He was holding the thing close to his face, whispering to it. He'd hold it out, run up the sidewalk past Mrs. Battaglia's house, and circle back, dipping his hand up and down as if he were flying one of our Balsa wood airplane models.

"Vroom," Liam said, running past me, arms extended.

As he raced past me again, I wrapped my arms around him, stopping him. "Liam," I said. "Drop that thing."

Liam smiled. "Playing a game," he said.

The dead crow was inches from my face. I released Liam and swatted at his hands. The crow fell to the sidewalk. It was fat and black and dead, with milky eyes like dull dimes.

I thought Liam was going to cry. His lips quivered for an instant, and he wiped his runny nose. He composed himself, stamped a foot and glowered at me.

"No fair," Liam said. "I was playing." He glanced down, toed the sidewalk with a sneaker, and whispered. "You never play with me."

The air went out of me. A ball of pain bloomed in my chest.

It was true. I'd spent my days with my comic books, or with Mrs. Battaglia. I'd wandered aimlessly from one end of the town to the other. From the black mill to the train tracks. Very rarely would Liam accompany me.

I tottered forward, grabbed Liam in a bear hug, squeezed. My breath hitched. Stinging tears sprang to my eyes. "I'm sorry, Liam. I didn't know."

Liam pushed me away. His face was red, scrunched up. His body trembled. His eyes watered. Anger and pain etched his features. I thought he was going to say something. But he turned, walked slowly up the front yard and into the house, his silence a heavy, accusatory weight in my chest.

Turning, I kicked the crow. It rolled into the dry gutter, black and dead and forgotten.

I stood on the sidewalk in a sticky summer silence, blinking. The town was a vast void, the life sucked out of it. The ache in my chest dulled. A small piece of me died that day. Each day since, I've been dying a little more.

ରୋଷ

Dad worked at the mill. I rarely saw him. He worked long hours, odd shifts. Most of the time I didn't know if he was at home, sleeping, or at work. He was an elusive wraith.

That pattern continued throughout my teens and early twenties, until my father died cold and alone in a squalid rooming house in Halifax, barely 50-years-old. His enigmatic presence was gone. But it haunts me still.

During that summer on Cumberland street I'd wander down to the mill, stand outside the gated chain-link fence, fingers hooked between the cold metal, face pressed tight to the fence, and peer at the black building. I would watch the thick black smoke from the chimney curl into the sallow, pewter sky. I'd listen for the horn that sounded a shift change, and watch as lines of sad, soot-covered, black-garbed men slowly ambled into and out of the black beast; indistinguishable shadows, marching with ant-like precision. I couldn't tell if my father was among them. Even here he was a ghost.

Liam never came down to the mill. I badgered him about it, but he wouldn't budge.

"Come on Liam," I'd say. Then I'd punch him in the arm. "You big pussy."

Liam would wipe the snot from his face. "I don't wanna go down there. Leave me alone." He'd developed a strange wheeze, a wet cough. 'Leave' came out sounding like 'leash.' His pink face seemed snottier than usual.

We'd walk the other way, up Cumberland, past the Canadian National rail yards. I was making a concerted effort to spend more time with my baby brother. We'd turn on to Huston street, near the end of town, and walk past Canada Meat Packers; a large grey processing plant that smelled of singed hair and cold dread. You could hear the hogs inside the plant shuffling and snorting in confusion. I imagined their fat pink bodies pressed tightly together in a dark room of blood and sawdust. The train tracks ran past the processing plant, and the hogs were shunted in by rail, day and night. Sometimes, at night, in my tiny bedroom on Cumberland, I heard their distressed wails carried on the sticky summer night wind. And mother wondered why I always left the bacon untouched on my plate.

At the end of Huston street was a tiny copse of trees. Through the trees was a meadow and a small dark pond. At the edge of the pond we would look for little flat stones to skip across the still surface of the water.

Liam could bounce a stone across the water with ease. It would skip eight, nine times before settling and dropping into the dark water. My stones, inevitably, would hit the surface, bounce once, then plop into the water, sinking like a dead thing, sending concentric ripples across the dark water.

"Did you see that?" Liam would ask, sending a stone skimming across the pond. He was wheezing, and 'see' sounded like 'she.' He'd jump up and down. A wide grin would split his pink face. It was good to see him smile.

One sweaty summer day I sat at the edge of the pond and watched Liam root around for stones, then skip them easily across the water, little sparkly droplets, briefly alive, rising from the surface. Liam stopped and stood staring out at the pond. He crouched, looked down.

"I see me," Liam said.

I stood, walked over to where he was bent. "What?" I asked.

Liam pointed. "There, in the water. I see me. Like a mirror."

I gazed down. Liam's wavering pink face was reflected in the water. "Yes," I said. "I see it."

Then I glanced to my own reflection. I saw a pallid face. It wasn't mine. It was some other me.

Liam dropped a stone into the water, shattering my reflection, my other me. He laughed. "I broke you."

I smiled. "You did, you bugger. You smashed me." I raised a mock fist. "I ought to smash you back."

Liam stepped into the pond. I lowered my hand. "What are you doing?" I asked.

He bent, plunged his arm into the water, pulled a rock from the bottom of the pond. His grin was infectious. "See," he said, holding the wet stone. "Mine." He pocketed the rock. "I'm going to keep this one."

"Why?" I asked.

Liam's grin widened. "So I can break you again."

03&0

Mid-summer and Liam's cough had gotten worse. He stayed inside, in his bedroom, with his comics and crayons. I'd walk up to his bedroom door, press my ear against the wood and listen. I could hear faint rustlings, like the unfolding of a newspaper. I could hear tiny, wet coughs. I'd rap on the door. Liam would grunt. "Go away." Other times he wouldn't say a word. His cough was answer enough.

I'd stare at the door, then move on, wondering what Liam was doing alone in his room. I'd saunter down to the pond or the mill or the train tracks. Visit Mrs. Battaglia, to eat sticky buns and drink sweet cold lemonade.

"Where is your brother?" Mrs. Battaglia asked one day, spooning extra sugar into her lemonade. Her drink was thick and murky and yellow, mimicking the colour of the air.

I could see Liam's bedroom window from that vantage point on her porch. I stared at the window. It was dark and cloudy like the mirror in our front hallway. Opaque. If I learned anything that summer, it was that the world would continue to be a dark mystery. An opaque mirror.

I pulled my gaze from the window and turned to Mrs. Battaglia. She smiled expectantly. "He's home," I answered. "He's not feeling well."

Her smile drooped. She stood, beckoned me to follow her. "Come," she said, and turned and walked into her house.

I stepped into the house. It was bright and airy, smelled of lemons. At the end of the hallway was a short mantel. Mrs. Battaglia stood at the mantel, her hands twisted up into the folds of her summer dress.

On the mantel was a vase of dried flowers, smelling of lilac. On either side of the vase sat two framed photographs. Mrs. Battaglia raised a fleshy hand, pointed. "That's Nino," she said. "The summer he died."

I moved closer, squinted. The photo showed a lean, handsome man sitting in an iron and wicker chair on a small porch. The same chair and porch I shared with Mrs. Battaglia. I gulped, nodded dully.

"And this," she said, hand caressing the dark wood of the frame, "is Joey. My little Joey. The summer that *he* died." Mrs. Battaglia stepped back, regarded the portraits with a look of stark sadness that nearly broke my heart. She said, "These are my summer ghosts."

I looked at the portrait of the young boy. It was a photo of me. Or Liam. Or any number of innocent, fair-haired, wide-eyed youths with big eyes and bigger smiles. I remembered Mrs. Battaglia's befuddled answer when I asked if she had any children.

Yes. Well, no.

"I'm sorry," I said. And it seemed I was always saying sorry that summer.

Mrs. Battaglia smiled humorlessly. "It's okay Jerry. It's all right." She smoothed the wrinkles out of her dress. "You should leave."

"Okay," I said.

"Forever," Mrs. Battaglia said. "You should leave this place. It isn't good for you. It isn't good for your brother. It isn't good for anyone."

"What about you?"

"I have nothing else, Jerry." She gazed at her dead husband and dead son. "My boys are here." She fixed me with a pleading stare. "Leave."

"Okay," I repeated. "Okay." I turned and stepped out of the house and onto the porch. I looked up at our dead grey house. There was Liam, at his window, watery face peering at me. Pudgy. Pinkish. Eyes wide, unblinking, intelligent. He looked, I imagined, like one of those hogs at the plant, trapped in a dark room, waiting. I smelt it on the air – fear and singed hair.

Inexplicably, a bolt of anger shook me. If I had a stone I would have hurled it at him. I'd have broken him like he'd broken me that day at the pond.

I wanted to shatter something.

CRSO

The day Liam died started like any other.

Me and mom were alone at the kitchen table, having breakfast. Liam was in his room. Dad was sleeping. I'd caught a brief glimpse of him through the kitchen window, a dark blur, as he came home from the mill.

I'd eaten my toast, picked at the eggs. I'd covered the bacon with a napkin and shoved it aside.

"I'm going out," I told mom.

She took a drag from her menthol cigarette, stared at the daily word jumble in the newspaper. "Fine," she said. "Don't be getting into mischief."

"Fine," I answered back, sharply.

She glanced up, put the newspaper down. "Mind you're quiet when you come home," she said. "Wouldn't want you to wake father. He'd be none too pleased."

I turned, stomped through the kitchen, down the hallway and past the dark mirror. I stepped outside, deliberately slammed the door shut.   Something caught my eye. I glanced up at Liam's bedroom. Briefly, a pale blur marred the dark window, then dissipated like smoke.

Mrs. Battaglia was sweeping her front sidewalk. She stopped whisking the imaginary dirt, waved. I didn't feel like talking, so I scurried down the walkway, headed toward the mill. I didn't acknowledge her. My anger was a hot stone in my chest.

The black mill belched fat black smoke. I stood at the rusty fence, gazed at the ashen sky. The curling smoke was hypnotic. The air was electric, and smelled of charred things.

A clattering noise drew my attention. I turned.

Through the yellow fog a fat pink-white hog dashed down Cumberland, straight at me.

A black van roared over the crest of the hill. The hog scuttled nearer, eyes wide, black, scared. It shot past me, hooves clattering on the cracked pavement, and smashed into the fence. It fell, stunned, then righted itself and stood quaking in the shadow of the mill. The reek of dread stung my nostrils.

The van screeched to a halt. The doors popped open and two men in blood-smeared coveralls jumped from the truck. Each man carried a long rust-stained hook.

The hog screamed—a forlorn wail—stared at me wide-eyed. I stuttered forward but one of the men brushed past me, shoved me out of the way with a blue-gloved hand. The men approached from either side and the hog tried to bolt between them. The big hooks reached out, caught the hog in its flanks and held the twisting, squealing beast in place. Blood trickled down the hog's side. The men dragged the crying animal along the pavement, hooks gouging pale pink flesh, and levered it into the back of the black van. Then they were gone, riding up Cumberland, past my house, back to the slaughterhouse. All they left behind was a thin trail of weak blood.

Shaken, I wandered up the street, to the front of my house. The town was silent, as if it were already dead. No one, not even jolly Mrs. Battaglia, was in sight. I looked up at Liam's bedroom window, but it was dark and cloudy and empty. Like me.

I slipped up the pitted walkway and crept into the house. I wasn't sure why I needed to be stealthy. The house settled. Old wood groaned. I smelled menthol cigarettes, burnt toast and fried eggs.

Heart askew, I started up the stairs. I stopped midway, turned and faced the mirror. That's when I saw me. The real me. Not the skinny, scared eight-year-old. In the mirror's cloudy depths, I was a grey old man with liver spots and stringy white hair. Trapped. What I was to become. What I already was.

Turning, I tiptoed up the stairs. I went to Liam's door, leaned against the thin wood, listened. Nothing. I knocked lightly. No answer.

"Liam," I whispered. "Liam."

I gripped the doorknob, turned, slowly pushed the door open.

The room was dim and dry. Thin grey light leaked through the window. Liam was on his bed. His face was turned toward me, eyes closed.

And I knew he was dead.

My heart stopped. I tottered forward, to the edge of the bed, stared down at that small, pale, dead face. A thin line of blood had trickled from Liam's nose, dried to the colour of weak tea. I thought of the hog, blood on its haunch.

A hot scream welled in my throat. I stifled it. I blinked and a flood of tears cascaded down my face. I got on the bed, stretched out beside Liam, put an arm around him, and sobbed quietly into his cooling body. My chest stung, as if my heart exploded, sending pointy shards into my torso. I dozed.

When I woke the room was still grey and dull, pallid light seeping through the cloudy window. It seemed I'd slept only a few minutes, but it was longer, because Liam was cold and stiff.

I stood, stared at Liam's blue-pale skin. One hand was curled into a tiny fist. I bent, slowly peeled back Liam's stiffening fingers. In the palm of his hand was a tiny dark stone. The stone he'd used to break me. The stone he threatened to use on me.

So I can break you again.

He'd gotten his wish. He'd broken me.

I plucked the tiny stone from his tiny hand. It was hot, as if it held all his body's dying heat.

Pocketing the hot stone I turned, walked out of the dim room, out of the dark house and into the thick monochrome world. The mill was black and silent. I trudged up Cumberland, past Mrs. Battaglia's house, over the hill, past the rail tracks, and stopped at the slaughterhouse.

I stood at the house of the dead and screamed a hot scream.

 os8o

The house still stands, barely. It is large and grey and silent, clutching tightly to past glories. A sad summer ghost. The tiny lawn is choked with thorny weeds, obscuring the walkway. The small porch has caved in. There's a hole in the roof, and the eaves-trough dangles precariously, swaying in the yellow wind.

I trudge through the thick weeds and step gingerly up onto the porch. Miraculously, it holds my weight. I step up to the door. A pair of two-by-six boards have been nailed across the doorway, forming a crude X. I reach up, grab the end of a board and pull. The rotted wood pulls easily from the frame, leaving behind two rusty nails. The other board is a bit more difficult, but I manage to yank it free with a few sharp tugs.

I push on the door and it swings in with a sharp hiss. The front hallway is dark. I step into the house and wait for my eyes to adjust.

There's no need to climb the stairs. I'm not 12 anymore. So I walk down the hallway and stop in front of the mirror. It's still there, as I knew it would be.

I gaze into the mirror. There's a boy in the mirror. Trapped.

The boy in the mirror is Liam. The boy in the mirror is little Joey Battaglia. And the boy in the mirror is me. It's all of us. Little dead ghost boys. Memories of a long ago summer. Because that's all that memories are, really. Ghosts. And that's all that I have left to me. Memories.

And ghosts.

I reach into a pocket and pull out the stone. Liam's stone. It is hot to the touch, as if fevered. I step back, lift my arm. My body trembles. A cough works its way into my throat. I hack and wheeze, spit yellow-green phlegm. I throw the stone at the mirror.

The mirror cracks, shatters.

I'm still broken, but no longer trapped.

SEA OF ASH AND SORROW

Since that day in New York, that day of grey ash and sorrow, when it rained white dust, he'd been looking. There was a black hole in him. Parts of him were missing. He'd lost something.

Maybe everything.

He searched amid the ruins, picking through the dust-covered detritus, shambling through empty office buildings and dark corridors as the fine dust coated him in a gritty film. He was moving through a sea of ash. A sea of ash and sorrow. A ghost-white specter moving among the dead.

Gradually, under the weight of his dust and ash cloak, he found clues, fragments of a puzzle: a piece of dry driftwood, a red plastic toy sailboat, silver-green fish scales. Memories stirred, danced like seaweed in a vast verdigris ocean.

Montauk!

As a child he visited Montauk. He'd walk the beach, collecting seashells and driftwood. He'd eat stale hotdogs and watch the blue-green surf; breathe in the heady, briny air. He'd sit and watch the white-capped waves, listen to their dark call—phlup... phlup—wonder about their languid pull.

The sea held him in thrall. The sea frightened him.

A memory bubbled up: A girl, bleach-blond hair, hazel eyes, alabaster skin, and a quicksilver smile. A day at the beach. Laughter and sun and cold Coca-Cola. Hot sand and blue, blue sky. An electric kiss behind the refreshment stand. She pulled away, slipped into the sea, swam out farther and farther, beckoning.

He stood rigid, watching her blond hair bob above the waves. Watching her turn, wave. He was mute, frozen, unable to do anything but stare at her receding form. He blinked, and she was gone. Gone.

As if she never existed.

He'd been searching for her ever since.

He held the memory, wouldn't let it sink to the dark depths of his mind, began to walk.

Mile after mile after grey mile, he marched. The cloak of ash weighed upon him. The gritty grey film of dust rubbed his skin raw. Penance. He thought of the sea, the cold obsidian waves, wondered if they would wash him clean like holy water.

On he walked. Cresting a hill, the sea came into view—a roiling, dark thing. The bone-white finger of beach kept it at bay. He moved across the sand, stood at the shore, peered at the horizon.

Nothing. The sea was vast, empty.

He took a tentative step. Then another. Another. The water was cold comfort. Unafraid, he swam. The ash washed off. Legs kicking, arms pumping, he churned through the brackish water. He looked back. The beach was gone. Like everything. So he swam and swam, until his arms complained, until his legs grew heavy, until his spirit weakened. Until he began to slip under and gulp down water, drifting down, down.... With a final, resolute push, he heaved up.

And there she was.

Her blond hair fanned out in the water. He smiled, reached for her, held her close.

And kissed her blue, blue lips.

THE MAN WHO ATE MOTHS

Every guilty person is his own hangman.
  – *Seneca*

His closets hold secrets: a noose, and a cage of moths.

Marc breeds moths in his bedroom's walk-in closet. They live in a large glass box with screened holes for ventilation. A cage. Like his apartment.

Marc oversees each stage of the moth's development, from egg, to larvae, to pupa, to moth. At night, before bed, he visits the moths. He considers himself a lazy *Lepidopterist*. Marc steps into the closet, flicks on the overhead light, opens the door of the glass cage. Like the moths, Marc is naked except for the fine silky hair covering his body. The moths stir, lift from branches or the side of the glass cage, and fly up to circle the wan light of the bare bulb. Their drone is music to his ears. Marc smiles, reaches up, snatches a couple moths from the swirling vortex, holds them loosely in his shaking hands. One moth is large grey-brown, the other smaller, cream and brown, and dappled with spots of pale yellow. Marc lifts his hands to his mouth and sucks the moths in. He swallows without chewing. The moths join the chorus of moths he has previously swallowed, filling his stomach even as they eat away at him.

Sometimes he wishes he could fly away, like a moth, to the sun. Marc grins, watches the silky hair grow, emerge. Perhaps, one day, he'll get his chance.

CRWSO

Cyndy loved moths.

Each night, at dusk, Marc and Cyndy sat on the front steps of the apartment building and watched the moths; large and small; fuzzy brown, silky white and smooth cream. The colour of fresh-turned earth and rain-soaked clouds. The moths swooped down on the wrought-iron lamps bordering the building's staircase, and flitted madly around the yellow light, crashing their furry bodies into the glass lamp pane and falling to the ground. They'd get inside the lamp, dance around the light and then *bzzt!*—fall.

Cyndy would study the swirling ball of moths, listen for the tell-tale *thumps* and *bzzts*.

"Why?" she once asked, turning to Marc. "Why?"

Marc had shrugged. "Beats me. I guess they don't like the darkness."

Later, when Marc found Cyndy's body, he asked the same question: "Why?"

CRWSO

The noose waits.

At 5 a.m. Marc eats breakfast: bacon and eggs, toast and coffee. It tastes like nothing at all. Bland. Empty. Like him. Like a lot of things.

At 5:20 a.m., Marc cleans away the breakfast dishes. His thoughts turn to Cyndy, and the noose that hangs, waiting, in his closet. It is a real noose, made of thick, heavy rope; twisted and braided. He walks to the hallway closet—his fine and private place—opens the door. The closet is bare but for a stool, and the noose hanging from the reinforced coat rack. The noose sways slightly in the sudden current caused by the opening of the door. It's as if the rope is waving a greeting. And, in a way, it is. Marc steps up on the stool

116

and places his head in the noose. He adjusts the slipknot, and carefully—so the knot doesn't snap his neck—steps down from the stool. His feet dangle inches from the floor. His eyes stare straight ahead, into the gloom of the small room. The rope bites and scratches his skin, tightens around his neck, slowly chokes off his air. His body twitches, feet kick. A low buzzing drone reaches his ears. The sound of tiny wings beating and flapping. And then he can feel the wings; some silky smooth; some furry, brushing his face, inviting him to their dance. His head feels like it is expanding, like a crazy clown carnival balloon, to the point of bursting. When darkness creeps into his vision, closes all around him like a blanket of brown moths, he gathers his remaining strength and, shaking, clambers back onto the stool. He loosens the noose, slips from its grip, and collapses to the floor, winded, barely conscious.

Marc wonders, as he always does, lying there with his breath hitching and his head pounding, how it felt for Cyndy, in those terror-stricken moments, when those hands squeezed, squeezed, squeezed....

But Cyndy died.

Marc doesn't want to die.

Dying is too good for Marc.

Marc pads to the bathroom, stares into the mirror, stares into his dark, hooded eyes, looking for someone who isn't there anymore. And his eyes trail to his throat, take in the livid, raw circle that rings his neck. A mark, a sign, a scarlet necklace of his own design. His fingertips dance, Braille-like, along the purple rut, and, briefly, ever briefly, Marc smiles. His eyes wander down his pale body. His torso and legs are completely covered in fine blonde-white hair, in silk. Marc turns, goes to his bedroom and gets dressed, choosing, as he always does, a turtleneck.

It is raining today, so Marc puts on a raincoat, leaves the apartment, goes outside.

Often, he sees Cyndy in the rain.

Marc wakes early so he can see the ghosts. At dusk they roam the city streets. They are like the grey mist and moist steam rising from subway grates; amorphous, elusive, inconsequential.

That is when he sees Cyndy, at dawn, the birth of a new day, wandering the streets she never got to wander while alive.

Cyndy died the day he tasted love. He was thirteen. Cyndy was eight.

Marc was in Marla Clarke's bedroom, his body electric, his lips tasting her lips, his hands under her shirt, rubbing, rubbing.

Cyndy, his sister, was lying in the stairwell of their building, as if asleep. Moths capered in the air above her. She'd been strangled. Livid handprints ringed her tiny, broken neck. A red necklace.

Marc wanted to crawl away and hide in a dark place, find a cocoon.

CRSO

Marc likes ghosts. They are like him. Existent but inconsequential.

He likes seeing Cyndy.

Early morning is the best time to see ghosts. There is a certain quality to the light, a clear view to another world, where, for several moments, nothing is transparent, nothing hidden. He stands on the sidewalk, or sits on the front steps, smoking the day's first cigarette, clutching a cup of black coffee, waiting for the world to come alive.

And he sees the ghosts.

Marc can't tell if they are coming or going. The ghosts shift silently through the shadows, moving easily along the rain-slicked streets, through fog-enshrouded parks. They look like everyone, anyone—young, old, fat, thin, hairy, bald—except muted, faded, like an old photo left too long in the sun. The ghosts walk past, ignoring him, their faces stoic, sad, indifferent. Sometimes, when it rains, Cyndy strolls past. And Marc's heart breaks. Tiny Cyndy. Eight years old. Forever eight. She doesn't see him. Doesn't look his way. She walks past, looking straight ahead, her pale face blank, looking lost; wearing the same blue jeans, the same striped top, the same bright white sneakers she'd worn all those years ago. A lost little girl.

She still has the scarlet bruises on her neck.

He never follows Cyndy, never tries to talk to her. What would he say? What *could* he say? I love you. I miss you. I'm sorry.

And the truest statement of all: I'm a failure.

Besides, he doesn't want to chase after her, doesn't want to communicate with her. It might break the spell, the enchantment. He might lose her forever. It's enough that he can see her, his Cyndy, in the rain.

Marc likes it out here, in the grey of the early morning twilight.

Just him and the ghosts.

He is still here, in the same apartment building. The one Cyndy lived—and died—in. His parents lived and died here, as well. But they were old, and had lived their lives as fully as they could. Simple lives that played out like so many others. Not like Cyndy's life. She never got to grow up. Never got to taste love. Of course, after that day at Marla Clarke's—trudging up the stairs, giddy, whistling, and finding pale, pretty Cyndy, thinking she was asleep, knowing she couldn't be, seeing the marks on her neck—he never again tasted love. What was the point? The people you loved died on you. It was a given.

It was raining the day he found Cyndy. A soft warm wind gusted. He walked home, reveling in the soft spatter of the drops, lifting his face to feel the cool rain. Puddles gathered on sidewalks, wet secrets waiting to be explored. The sun poked through the grey clouds in tiny golden shafts, and it seemed as if the rain was falling in slow motion, seemed as if the sun caught it, like a prism, and the rain refracted into hundreds of tiny diamonds, sparkling, shining just for him.

Magic!

Like Cyndy in the rain.

When he found her in the dark stairwell, when he realized she was gone, he didn't know what to do. There was a hollow black pit in his stomach, as if his innards were slipping away. So he sat with her, and held her hand, and stroked her hair. Stared at the bright red ring circling her neck. Stared at the swirling, mad moth dance.

And he wept.

Marc watched the frolicking moths, watched their melancholic dance. He snatched one from the air, a delicate white thing, and held it in cupped hands. He opened his hands slightly, peeked at

119

the moth. Its wings shuddered, antennae bristled. Pale blond hair, like silk, trailed from the moth's body. Marc leaned close, brought the moth up to his face, and popped it in his mouth. It fluttered for a long time in his mouth, bouncing from top to bottom, side to side, and then quieted.

And Marc swallowed the moth. It tasted like nothing.

He felt the moth in his belly, he was sure of it, flying, fluttering; a strange butterfly ballet. The moth settled.

And began to feed.

CR80

They thought he did it, of course. Thought he strangled Cyndy. Thought he killed his sweet little sister, a girl with eyes the colour of smoke and mystery, with hair the colour of straw and fire.

But the ligature marks didn't match his hand size.

Of course they didn't. He didn't kill her. At least not in the real sense. But he wasn't home, watching Cyndy, keeping an eye on his little sister. Instead, he was at Marla's house, trying to get in her pants. Trying to taste her love.

CR80

Outside, on the cold grey steps, Marc lights a cigarette. He blows a stream of blue smoke into the wet air, watches it curl and twist, waver and dissipate, fall apart like so many other things.

He waits. And he hopes. His stomach aches. The moths use their mandibles, their proboscises, to tear chunks from his flesh, to suck nutrients from his stomach lining. To feed. To live. Slowly they eat away at him. He is becoming—if he already isn't— a hollow man.

And there she is, Cyndy, rounding a corner and walking steadfastly up the street, through the grey drizzle, her pig-tails swaying. She stares straight ahead—blank, unblinking China doll eyes. Cyndy glides past the steps, and Marc stares at her, at the raw, red ring circling her neck. He shudders, suppresses a moan, and tries a smile. All he can manage is a crooked grin. And Cyndy is gone, past the apartment, up the street, disappearing into the pearly mist, a great grey hand closing around her, squeezing.

Shaking, Marc drags on his cigarette and flicks it to the wet curb. He watches the blue smoke curl and die, watches the tiny orange ember wink out.

Sometimes, Marc imagines Cyndy turning to him, her face pale blue-white, slack, her eyes like faded chunks of coal, her mouth opening, closing, opening, closing, speaking, her voice alternately a whisper and a scream. *"Don't do it. Don't do it, Marc."*

What? Marc thinks. Don't do what?

Don't leave me, Marc.

Too late.

Just his imagination, though. There is no voice on the wind. No whisper. No scream. Of course, Marc imagines a lot of things. Sometimes, when he opens the door to his closet he imagines Cyndy is in there, waiting, hanging limply from the corded rope, her neck twisted, her face a milky blue. Moths flutter madly around her head; brown feathery wings brushing her face. She winks at Marc. Her lips slowly curl, smiling the smile of a dead eight-year-old child.

The emptiness eats away at his insides.

CRES

In his hand is a large black moth, each wing spotted with a big white dot like some great seeing eye. Marc strokes the moth's wings. He strokes the fine blonde silk covering his body. The glass cage rattles and shakes as the moths fly. The air buzzes, thrums like an electrical field. The flap of many frenzied wings adds another note to the strange discordant din.

Marc's stomach flutters, roils. They are inside him, churning, seeking release. He lifts the large moth, sucks it into his mouth. He swallows. Then he grabs another moth, a furry grey one, and pops it into his mouth. Swallows. Both hands reaching now, left and right, he pulls moths from the air—pearly white, dishwater brown, lemon yellow and dappled gold—shoves them in his mouth and gulps them down, filling the void even as they eat and eat.

121

Marc stumbles to bed, his head buzzing, his stomach rumbling. He lies down on his side, stretches his legs straight out. As night wears on, the delicate silk grows longer, wraps around him, protectively, encasing him. Some of the threads wrap around his neck, like a noose. His vision fades, winks out.

He lies in the darkness, wondering what will emerge.

Twilight in the Field of Forever

(with Carol Weekes)

The pale little girl scampered across the weed-choked meadow.

Somewhere distant a cicada sang. *Genus Magicicada*. The seventeen year locust. Though, truth be told, it wasn't a true locust. There was a time when I liked the cicada's song. Seventeen years, I thought. How apt.

I saw her in the field across from the abandoned textiles building which had shut down nearly two decades ago in the meadow that ran beside it for as far as the eye could see. The field of forever, as I liked to call it. The sun had begun to set, bathing the clearing in honey glow. She was tiny, running imp-like among the grass and heather, pigtails flying, kicking up dust from her heels in the soft, dry dirt. Funny, I thought, I'd never seen her here before. Nor had I noticed her in the neighborhood, and I knew everybody from around town.

When I got closer and chanced a peek from around the abrasive surface and circumference of a massive oak, I caught her staring back at me open-mouthed and wide-eyed, no doubt stunned at my ruined, lumpy face. I pulled back, using the tree to hide, my chest heaving. I waited until it seemed as if the day itself held its breath to watch what might happen next, then poked my head around the tree.

She was gone.

The field was empty, save for a single butter-yellow moth twisting and flitting across the tops of the wild flowers. Twilight descended like a grey cloak, draining the last of the sun from the sky and throwing the field and distant building into shadow, its windows dark square holes.

I stepped out from my cover and squinted into the distance. I could see the opening to a street that would eventually lead into the residential section of town. No little pig-tailed girl with her chestnut hair that shone the colour of clear maple syrup. She had vanished. The droning buzz of a lonely cicada remained the only sign of life around me now.

Sometimes... sometimes the cicada screams.

A chill crossed over my flesh. I folded my arms across themselves in an attempt to try and warm myself. Suddenly, a faint sound from behind me. My ears prickled.

It came again louder, and I recognized it for what it was: a child's laughter, gleeful, mocking, a most definite taunting sound, the patchwork of thorns and brambles rubbing along each other's surface.

I turned and saw her, aiming an idle kick at the ground with a black patent-leather shoe. A cloud of dust festooned the air around the base of her toe. Through waning twilight, she tossed me a shy, coy smile. Or perhaps it was more of a mischievous grin.

She stopped kicking the dirt as abruptly as she'd started. The smile slipped from her face, her young mouth forming into a look too serious for her age. She uttered "Boo."

Goose bumps jumped up along my skin. I stepped back, hugging myself tighter. The thrill of her presence when I had never heard her creep up behind me, when I thought for certain she'd run off in the direction of town, (and how she could have circled around without my seeing her, short of her crawling low through the picky texture of grass) created a sensation of Halloween style shivers. She laughed again, the smile returning. I heard her voice carry and echo from different points of the field.

"Don't be afraid," she told me, her eyes roaming my face, inspecting the red ruin. "I won't hurt you. My name is Kaylee."

My hand flew up, rubbed the knobby scar tissue. "I-I'm not afraid. You just startled me a bit."

"I'm sorry. I like to play. Do you still like to play too? I wish I knew someone who would visit me here more often."

She was pretty in a sad, almost empty kind of way. I wondered if she suffered from bullying in school, asking a woman of my age, seventeen, (and instantly I thought of the Genus Magicicada) with a hideous disfigurement, if I'd still like to play. The truth was no, I didn't engage in the act of play anymore, and perhaps that's part of the dull patina of adolescence--how quickly we forget the spontaneity of our own childhood. Besides, I was too old and too ugly. Yet here was this wisp of a girl, standing wraith-like in this field of forever, asking me if I'd like to play with her. I was secretly thrilled. How long had it been since I'd had anyone to play with? To talk with? She inspired me.

"Yes," I said. "I can play with you, Kaylee." I felt determined to please her, more afraid to hurt her feelings.

She wore a frilly dress, a bit out of style, but perhaps the family was poor and shopped in the local thrift stores; you took what was in good condition regardless of style. I'd had a similar dress myself back in an era when little girls could play alone in fields with strangers without worrying about who they may be talking to. White socks contrasted
her black shoes, ending at the ankles. She looked as if she hadn't seen a lot of sun in a while. She was covered in a fine film of dust, giving her an ephemeral appearance. A facade. But I had a keen eye. I had learned to be observant. I could see beyond the grime.

"Have you been playing in that old factory over there? I see you've gotten your dress dirty. It's dangerous in there, you know." My face itched and I rubbed it. "That's why the town has boarded up most of its windows, although I know some of the older local children have broken inside to fool around. I've been in there once before, a long, long time ago." I smirked. "Why are you out here alone? Won't your parents worry?"

"No," she said. "I'm allowed to do as I please."

"That's the problem these days," I echoed, more to myself than to her. "Well then, what kind of game shall we play? Only for a for few minutes, mind you, and then I shall walk with you to see you home safe." I looked up. The world was slate-grey, colorless and pale. "It'll soon be dark," I added.

125

Her smiled faltered now. "I'm not allowed to walk with strangers."

"Oh? But you're allowed to talk and play with them? Does that make a lot of sense to you?"

Her face adopted a quizzical expression. "Let's play hide and seek," she said as if not wanting to spoil the moment any further. "It's my favorite. I often play it here in the field."

"With who?" I asked.

She looked at me blankly. "Friends."

Yet, I could not picture her with other children her age. She was different. The outsider. I envisioned her alone, haunting this field daily, looking for adventure.

"Fine," I said. "I'll count first and you can hide."

Her eyes crinkled mischievously. Then she was off and running, the space she had occupied empty as if she hadn't been there.

I chortled, turned and ran to my favorite tree, its thick, century-old branches twisting and coiling out from its main trunk like distended hands reaching toward the sky. My feet flew over the bone-dry ground, hardly touching. In the rising moonlight I noticed how pale my flesh looked--almost transparent. Again came that sense: a chill from all directions and no direction at once. How could she feel so free to play with me? Where
was her fear? I was, after all, new to her, an unknown individual. For I was lonely too, a wandering entity trying to find myself in a world which never seemed to fit around me. I had been her at her age--alone and seeking friends. I'd since found my pleasure in quiet places of solitude. I came here to examine my thoughts and watch people from a distance, finding safety in being the observer, rather than the participant. Making friends with people of any age had never come easy, and likely never would for me. I didn't want to spoil this chance. I felt she was different. She wouldn't be like the rest of them.

I counted to ten behind the tree and then poked my head out again to discover her gone. Of course she would be, as the nature of the game demanded that she hide.

"I'm coming to find you," I called and began my descent into the field that was almost blue with twilight, and cool in its late summer breeze. The grasses remained silent as I passed in my quest to find her, determined not to let her down for I hoped she would return again tomorrow.

Somewhere distant a cicada cried. My fingertips reached up, traced the map-work of my face. If you listen carefully it sounds almost human. And people do scream. Fear and
pain will make you scream. I hope the little girl has never experienced fear or pain.

I trembled. I told myself that it was not a human that I'd heard. Not a winsome little girl in an empty field that stretched on forever.

There weren't many places for the child to hide; a few scant trees. Yet the grass was plenty high in places, and afforded a protection of sorts. The large dark hulk of the textiles building lurked on the far horizon. I shuddered. Surely she wouldn't go into that foul place. Would she? Besides, it was across the other side of the meadow and I'd have noticed the child's movements in the tall grass. She was clever but she was just a child after all, a thing of flesh and blood.

Smiling, I pushed into the tall grass, parting it with grand sweeps of my arms. A cool cinnamon-scented wind blew. I moved forward, gently, squinting into the murky milk-white world. The grass swayed, hypnotically. Perhaps, I dimly realized, I would not be able to discern the child's movements.

"Kaylee," I called. "Kaylee."

I continued through the field, trudging through the sedge, searching, peering. A sound reached my ears, a giggle, and the whispery, raspy sound of movement through the underbrush. Faint but growing, another sound, the cicada again.

The child was nowhere in sight. I hurried forward, my movements frantic. "<u>Kaylee!</u>" I screeched. "Kaylee," I called again, plunging ahead, straining for a glimpse of the pale, comely little girl.

I began to panic, stumbling forward, arms swinging, shouting her name. "Kaylee! Kaylee!" What if she'd hurt herself? She'd be all alone, tired and afraid.

Why wouldn't she answer me?

That scream again, high and piercing. Seventeen years. I continued on, unmindful of its cruel taunts. The air smelled of electricity and thrummed like a hundred power lines. The grass tugged and pulled at me, brambles nipping me, sticking to my clothing. I bulldozed my way through the tall, rough stalks, running, searching, crying out "Kaylee!"

Then I was thrown into darkness.

I looked up. The shadow of that twisted building loomed from on high, a dark hulking thing. My heart hammered and my face flushed crimson. I rubbed it instinctively. Sweat and goose bumps dotted my flesh. My mouth went dry. I tried to speak but all I could manage was a weak murmur.

"*K-Kaylee-e-e-e?*"

Then the world tilted and my head spun as the memory came flooding back:

A hot summer day, the cicada singing a melodious tune. Seventeen years old. Nothing to do but play in the field, skipping, hopping, rolling in the grass, climbing trees. Then coming upon the strange, silent building and stealing my nerves to sneak inside, pushing through an unlatched window, dropping to the floor, my eyes adjusting to the dim light, wandering through the machines, past the drums of foul-smelling liquid, fingers dancing along the string and fabrics. Then a creak or a groan, and I run, blindly, my heart pounding, the cicada's song now a scream reverberating inside my skull. I run, run, run, headlong into one of the drums, my body flipping, face splashing into the vat, and I scream and scream and scream because it hurts, it hurts so bad. Panicked, clawing at my face, I run for a door, pull it wide and rush headlong into the field, still screaming, high and strident. Running and running and running in the field of forever, until I tire, until I lay down on the soft earth, a sad drone in my head as the world leaks to twilight.

I blink, shake my head, forcing the memory away.

Genus Magicicada. The seventeen year locust. Seventeen years old. A stark abandoned building, left vacant seventeen years.

"Kaylee." A voice, not mine, calling the child.

128

"Boo!" I spin, and the child is standing before me with a fishhook smile.

"Scared you, didn't I?" Kaylee says.

"Yes," I answer.

Closer now. "Kaylee!"

Still smiling, Kaylee lifts a hand, waves. "You have to go now."

I return the smile. "Yes, and so do you."

A woman comes into view, marching across the field with bold purpose. "Kaylee," the woman calls, beckoning with a hand.

Kaylee turns, the smile slipping from her face.

The woman reaches her. "There you are, young lady. I've been looking all over for you." The woman looks up at the building. "It isn't safe here."

Kaylee stares.

"Who were you speaking to?"

"A friend."

The woman looks up, makes a show of scanning the area. "Nobody here, Kaylee, but you and the crickets."

"Cicada."

The woman crinkles a brow. "What?"

"Never mind," Kaylee said.

"Come," the woman said, tugging the child away.

Kaylee grinned, tossed a glance behind her. "I could stay here forever," she said, and then skipped off.

"Me too," I whispered and my voice was a soft wind that rustled in a twilight-bathed field that went on forever and ever. "Me too," I repeated, my voice was high and shrill. A mad cacophonous din, it droned and buzzed.

Somewhere among the golden fields a cicada screamed.

Seventeen, I thought. Always seventeen.

LAST TRAIN HOME

Phipps, briefcase in hand, slipped unobtrusively from the dark, empty office building and began the walk to the subway along rain-slicked streets. He was a slight, balding, bespeckled, nervous man who smiled rarely.

Christ, he thought, *Muriel's gonna kill me. Third time this week.* He'd phoned her, told her he was running late but he'd felt the stony silence and icy chill across the phone line. Much the same way he'd felt it in their bed.

Phipps looked around, hoping a taxi would be in sight, but the streets were empty. He checked his watch and cursed silently to himself. He'd have to hurry if he was going to catch the last train.

He quickened his pace, the heels of his shoes making muffled clopping sounds on the sidewalk. He stopped at an intersection, waiting for the red light to change.

Clop clop.

Phipps whirled around. *What was that?* The streets were dark, shadowy and desolate. He shrugged, turned back and proceeded to cross on the green light, wondering about the conditioned reflex that had made him stop at the barren intersection. We're creatures of habit, he thought.

Suddenly, a car sped by, tires hissing on the wet pavement, startling him. Phipps could just make out the lit FOR HIRE sign as the cab turned a corner and raced away. Fuck! He checked his watch again and began to run, his overcoat flapping like large, leathery bat wings. A fine, light drizzle misted his small, round spectacles and he had to stop a few times to wipe them clean.

Phipps reached the station, dumped a token into the slot and raced up the concourse just in time to fling himself into the closing doors of the departing train. He slumped into a seat, huffing and puffing, and looked up as the train was entering the tunnel to see a bright cyclopean eye staring at him from the opposite track. Then he was plunged into darkness.

CRIXD

Muriel was asleep when he got home. Or, at least she was going through the pretense of sleep as he looked into their bedroom. No bother. He didn't particularly relish the idea of talking to her at the moment.

Phipps sat down at the tiny table, in the tiny kitchen of their tiny apartment. A microwaved TV dinner sat congealing in front of him. He was thinking about what he saw in the subway and had rationalized it as just the workings of a tired mind and over active imagination. He ate half the beef pattie in gravy and went to bed.

He dreamt while he slept. Dreamt of large, ravening beasts with razor talons and spiked teeth lumbering through his office, tearing at white-shirted managers, ripping their flesh and swallowing large, steaming gobbets of sweet, pink meat.

CRIXD

The next morning at breakfast he told Muriel about the eye.

"An eye was it, Virgil?" Muriel taunted. "You sure it wasn't an ear? Or perhaps a nose," she said, smiling.

"Yes, of course, it wasn't real, dear. I was just telling you what I thought I saw. What it looked like."

"Puh-leeze," she said, biting into her toast.

"It winked."

"What?"

"It winked at me," repeated Phipps.

Muriel raised an eyebrow, looked at her husband. "Really, Virgil, you've got to stop working so late. You're confused, is all."

"I'm not confused, Muriel. Not at all. I know it wasn't real. Probably just a light of some kind. Train's going pretty fast, you know. I was just making conversation."

Muriel took a sip of Earl Grey, placed the cup in its chipped saucer and turned a page in The Enquirer. "Hmmph! Making conversation, he says. Perhaps if he were here at dinner time," she drawled, "he could make some conversation."

Virgil Phipps face reddened like a kid caught stealing candy. "I-I need to catch up, Muriel. It's a busy time. Besides, we could use the extra money."

"Oh, you noticed, did you? This ain't exactly the lap of luxury, Virgil."

"Goodbye, Muriel."

Phipps gathered his dishes, dumped them in the sink, grabbed his briefcase and went out the door to work.

ɔ℞ɛɔ

At the office, Adams was on his ass all day. Whenever Phipps cleared the paper from his desk Adams would drop another load on it.

"Here ya' go, Phipps. There's just no end to it." And Adams would saunter back into his office, smiling smugly, and shut the door.

Phipps thought Adams was doing it on purpose. He and Adams had both applied for the managerial job when it had come open. Adams had won out, and Phipps life had been hell ever since. At times Phipps would look up and see Adams peering out at him between the slats of his office blinds. He confronted Adams about it once.

"You nuts or something?" said Adams. Then a mean grin creased his florid face. "Or ya' just trying to make trouble? Cause trust me, you don't want no trouble from me, fancy boy."

After that Phipps rarely said anything to Adams.

During his lunch break Phipps went out to grab a hot dog from one of the many parasitical vendors that crowded the street corners like common carnival hucksters. He handed the swarthy man a ten but only got change for a fiver.

"I gave you ten," said Phipps.

The man smiled incredulously and held a five between greasy fingers.

133

Phipps reached over to grab the bill but the man pulled it back and sneered. "This," said the man, "is all you gave me. I know you. I know your tricks." He tucked the bill into his waist pouch, all the time smiling that silly smile.

Phipps took a bite of his hot dog, chewed it carefully for a moment and then spit it at the man, spraying the man's bib with chunks of meat and bun. "Bastard," said Phipps, storming back to the building and his tiny office cubicle.

At six o'clock Phipps was rising from his chair, making ready to leave, when Adams walked up, holding an armload of papers. He dropped the bundle on Phipps desk with a heavy thunk.

"Sorry, Phipps, but these gotta get processed tonight."

"Couldn't someone else do it?" asked Phipps. "I been late every day this week."

"Everyone else has got plans or has gone home, Phipps. Ker-rist! You think I'd ask you if I had a choice. Sorry, it's gotta get done and you're the man." Adams clapped Phipps on the shoulder. "You have a good night now, Virgil." He strode out the door, whistling.

Phipps sighed, sat down and got to work. Soon, the pile on his desk was substantially smaller. He was starting to feel good about himself until he realized he hadn't phoned Muriel. Oh, shit! he thought. He checked the time. Good, it wasn't so late she'd be asleep. He picked up the receiver and dialed. It rang and rang. He counted eighteen rings before he hung up. He dialed again, thinking perhaps he'd dialed wrong the first time. After a full twenty-five rings he gave up. Where was she? Was she just ignoring him? That was probably it, he thought. Getting back at him for some imagined wrong.

He hung up the phone and tried to work. Out of the corner of his eye he noticed the night janitor leaning on his mop, staring at him. Phipps looked up but the kid was just lazily sweeping the floor. But every time he turned back to his desk he thought he saw the kid stop his work to gawk at Phipps as if he were some circus freak.

Phipps attacked the remaining work on his desk, putting the janitor out of his mind, and finished it up in short order. Still, by the time he stepped out into the chill evening, it was quite late. He had time to make the train, though. No mad dash tonight.

Phipps cinched the belt on his overcoat and began the walk to the station. It was a crisp, cloudless night, the stars winking at him in some strange, symbiotic fashion.

Again, he was alone on the streets. Virgil Phipps, all alone.

Tonight, he didn't stop at the red light, just crossed against it, and a feeling of pure joy washed over him. A delicious little thrill coursed through him, as if that little illicit act had freed him from the days' monotony.

Suddenly, a figure stepped from the shadows, arms flailing madly, pawing at him. He felt a spray of liquid on his neck and the acrid scent of cheap wine assailed him.

"Spare some ch-change?" asked the man, the words making their way through a mouth hidden deep in the center of a nicotine-stained beard.

"Blimey, no, man. You scared the devil out of me. Shove off!" Phipps pushed away from the man and headed on his way. The little bit of good cheer he was experiencing deflated out of him like a burst balloon.

Upon reaching the station, Phipps grabbed a seat near the rear of the train. Being the final train, it would wait until its scheduled departure time, so Phipps had a few minutes to sit and relax.

From here, in the back coach, he could see the length of the track, into the opposite tunnel. He thought he saw a brief flash of light, as if a flashlight was turned on and quickly turned off again. Then a strange iridescent glow seemed to emanate from the tunnel, and Phipps thought he could make out a large, purple oval shape.

There was only one other patron in this part of the train and Phipps gestured to him. "Do you see that?" he asked.

"What? See what?"

"Down there, in the tunnel. Something weird."

The man got out of his seat and looked out the window to where Phipps was pointing. "I don't see nothing, bub."

"But you must. It's as plain as the nose on your face."

You been drinking?" asked the man.

"Course not," said Phipps.

"Smells like it," said the man, returning to his seat. "Don't bother me, you hear?"

The doors shut and the train began slowly to move. Phipps sat up in his seat and strained to see into the tunnel. As the train gained speed and moved closer to the tunnel entrance, the shape became more distinct. Just before he was thrown into darkness, Phipps thought he could make out three or four appendages on either side of what appeared to be an egg-shaped body. The arms-- for that is what he thought they were--seemed to wave at him in slow motion like sea plankton, beckoning him. For the first time in a long while Phipps was surprised to find himself smiling.

 C3&O

Muriel was waiting up for him when he got home. She was in the living room, sitting in the dark. When Phipps trod across the worn carpet she flicked on a lamp, surprising him.

"Not even the decency to call, Virgil?"

"I-I did call, Muriel. Several times I tried. There was no answer."

"I've been home all night, Virgil. Just like last night, the night before that, and the night before that. Like all the nights."

"You must believe me," pleaded Phipps.

"Must I?"

Phipps walked over to stand by Muriel. "Something must be wrong with the phone service. I tried, I did." He placed a hand placatingly on her shoulder. "Tell you what, when I'm finished this year end business we'll go away somewhere. Just me and you. Fancy a trip, do you, Muriel?"

"On your salary? Hah? We'd be lucky—What's that smell? Virgil Phipps!! You've been drinking!"

"I haven't, Muriel. I haven't. There was a wino, I didn't see him—"

"Enough, Virgil. I'm off to bed." She stood, brushing his hand of her shoulder the way she would a crumb. "You can sleep out here. Honestly, you act like a child, Virgil Phipps. Probably thankful we didn't have any, eh? *Couldn't* have any. Thankful you're sterile, aren't you?" And with that she stomped off to the bedroom, slamming the door behind her.

Virgil sat down on the couch and loosened the tie from around his neck. He ran a hand through thinning hair and sighed loudly. Probably for the best, he thought. Not like they really shared the bed anymore, anyway.

He remembered what it used to be like, before the tests, before the acrimony. Just two young kids in love. Two kids with a passion and heat that seemed destined to burn bright forever.

It wasn't always this way, he remembered. But after the sterility results, after numerous rejections for promotions, when it became apparent that he would probably be stuck where he is for the remainder of his working life, Muriel had lost interest. A better life is what she had wanted, one with small, innocuous children to take up her idle time with. A life she wasn't going to have. But Muriel Phipps hadn't the guts to leave.

Virgil leaned back on the couch and closed his eyes. Thank God tomorrow's Friday, he thought.

Again, he dreamed. This time he dreamt of large shadowy creatures that ran warm tendrils and moist tongues along his rigid body. Creatures that burned with a brilliant midnight heat and opened many inviting orifices, welcoming him in to their waiting, moist maw.

രുജ

Breakfast the next morning and Muriel was still in a mood.

"Any plans for today?" asked Phipps.

"No."

"Talk to your sister lately?"

"No."

"Think you'll be by the dry cleaners at all? I've some shirts need picking up."

"No."

"There's something in the tunnel, Muriel."

That got her attention. "What?"

The subway tunnel, there's something in it."

"Like what, Virgil, more eyes?"

He told her.

"Giant spiders, Virgil?" She laughed. "How much *did* you drink last night? Egg-shaped spiders lurking in the tunnels. And where were the little green men and the pink elephants? Perhaps at the next stop, eh, Virgil?"

Phipps lifted his mug and drained the last of his tepid coffee. His bacon and eggs sat untouched on his plate. He stood, dutifully bringing his dishes to the sink.

"Least you could do is wash up them dishes," said Muriel. "You've got time."

Phipps put some soap and water in the sink and began to wash the plates. It took both hands to wield the heavy cast iron frying pan. When he was done, he left for work. There was no need to say goodbye to Muriel.

CR&SO

Friday, and it was all Phipps could do to concentrate on his work. Surely what he'd seen hadn't been real. Had it? It was a trick of the light. Perhaps some workmen had left some equipment down there. Yes, that was it. Simple really. Probably doing repairs in another section of the tunnel.

Phipps saw Adams in the hallway just past lunch hour and waved him down. "It's about the janitor, sir," said Phipps. "He gives me the creeps."

Adams laughed. "Janitor? Janitor? You're a real kidder, you are, Phipps." Adams shook his head in wonder and continued on down the hall.

The rest of the day was a blur of numbers and equations and at six o'clock Adams smacked him sharply on the shoulder. "Let's go, Phipps. The weekend awaits."

Phipps looked up startled, then at the few papers littering his desk. He knew the work could wait 'til Monday but was surprised to find himself saying, "Just going to clear up these couple items. I'll be along shortly. You have a great weekend, Mr. Adams, sir."

Adams snorted. "Suit yourself. You're a strange bird, Phipps. A strange bird, indeed."

Adams left and Phipps was alone in the office. Forty-five minutes later he was finished his work, tapping the end of a pencil on his blotter and staring idly at the clock. His stomach growled in protest and he got up from his desk, put his coat on and left the building. What was he thinking? He laughed. Shit, this is nuts, I gotta get home, he thought.

Phipps took a seat in the middle of the train. The car was about half full and passengers on the other side waited with dull expressions for the westbound train.

Virgil.

He thought he heard his name, but it could have been the hiss of the closing doors.

Here, Virgil, in here.

The car lurched forward awkwardly, wheels whining and groaning on the rails.

Phipps stared blankly ahead, looking into the tunnel as the departing car jostled him. The creature was there, staring at him, its large bruise-colored body--moist and slick looking in the tunnel light--undulating to some hypnotic rhythm. There was a large red gash, like a sideways mouth, splitting its body, opening and closing, revealing sharp, crooked teeth that gleamed like stars in an inky night.

Phipps sat up, smiling, and pointed with shaking hands at the beast. A long, guttural sob escaped his lips and his body quivered with joy as darkness engulfed him.

CR80

He got home, half expecting Muriel to be waiting in the living room for him, but she was still at the kitchen table, where he'd left her.

"Hi," he said.

Nothing, she sat there, unmoving.

"Got home quick as I could, Muriel."

She stared at him, vacantly.

In one of her moods, he thought.

"Let's go to bed, Muriel. I know it's early, but we don't have to sleep," he said, a mischievous grin on his face.

He took her to the bedroom, undressed her and lay her down on the bed. He kissed and caressed her but she was cold, unresponsive.

139

Soon, he fell asleep.

CRSO

Phipps awoke a little while later, his hand sticky from where it had caught in her hair. He pulled it free, smoothed the hair back into place and washed his hand in the bathroom sink.

He checked the time and smiled. He had time to catch the train. The last train.

Phipps went over and kissed Muriel on the lips. "Night, dear. Sweet dreams." He closed her eyes.

Phipps went out the apartment door, flagged a cab and got out at the train station. He pushed a token into the slot, walked out onto the platform and waited. The train arrived, the doors opened, then closed, and the train departed.

Phipps stood, watching the train depart, then hopped down onto the tracks. He crossed over to the other track, carefully avoiding the third rail, and looked into the dark mouth of the tunnel. A glow came from passage, lighting his way, and he saw the beast staring at him.

The creature roared, shaking the ground, and he gleefully stepped forward, awaiting its sweet embrace.

WHEN CHILDREN WEEP

It was early spring, not the time of year for a proper holiday, Ian reckoned. But Emily was gone, the ache in his chest still fresh, and he felt the need to get away, if only to be rid of the slack-faced co-workers who shuffled up to him to mumble their self-effacing condolences.

And Ben, young Ben, sweet and blonde and motherless? What was he to do with Ben?

"Mum?" Ben had asked, eyes wide and watery.

"No," Ian answered, wanting to kiss away his tears, wanting to taste nature's bitter brine.

He would go to Grandview, he decided. Go back really, for he and Emily had initially met in the quaint seaside resort.

On the surface it seemed a decidedly bad place to visit once more. Why go rekindling those old memories? Yet, curiously, that is precisely what Ian wanted to do. He wanted to remember the good times. Didn't want to mope around the office or home, wallowing in self-pity, putting on airs for his family and friends. Wanted to remember Emily; her smile, her smell, her voice.

Oh, her voice! She would sing to him, as his mother had, soft and lilting in the murky twilight.

Oh, vast dark beauty; liquid jewel
Cool caliginous depths beckon; emerald waves seethe
Another soul flounders
Lost to the weed-choked Sargasso Sea.

So Grandview seemed just the tonic.

He started out early on Monday morning, Ben sitting quietly on the seat beside him. He hoped to get there by mid-afternoon, maybe in time for tea. It was a fine bright morning, and as he headed out he tuned the radio to a pop station and found himself whistling along to the innocuous music.

Ben stared straight ahead, silent, unsmiling. He tried talking to the boy, even tousled his hair at one point, but Ben was mute, uncommunicative. Truth be told, he never was much of a father to the child.

Ben was Emily's boy through and through. And, as he'd expected, the boy had grown sullen and serious once Emily was gone.

Ian himself had grown up an only child of a single parent. His father left them when Ian was but a toddler. His mother worked damn hard to put bread on the table, clean clothes on his back. It damn near killed her, Ian remembered. He wouldn't wish the same for anybody.

Ian looked over at the sad, lonely boy and sighed. Poor, poor Ben. Really, as Ian's mother often opined, what was a boy without his mother? Nothing.

They drove for several hours, stopping around noon to grab a quick ham and cheese. The boy used the bathroom, but only picked at his ketchup-doused french fries. When they started out again the sun disappeared behind great, grey clouds and the wind picked up. Sgt. Pepper blared from the tinny radio. A couple more hours and they'd be there.

As they drove, the weather became more inclement. The sky went from pewter to charcoal, the clouds fat and black. The wind howled and moaned, rocking the small car, and the radio lost its signal, producing nothing more than loud squawks and static. The radio hissed, yet underneath the garbled white noise Ian imagined he heard something else; a voice, soft, melodic, familiar. He cocked an ear, listened, listened. . .

...*Oh, sad Sargasso*...

...but the sound leaked away like air from a dying balloon.

When Ian turned the car onto the long driveway into Grandview the skies opened in a torrent, the rain lashing at them as they scrambled out the car and into the lobby. He had missed tea, more than likely.

Grandview was as he remembered. The foyer was wide and dim, the same flowered yellow wallpaper and pine wainscoting covering the walls. A few prints, mostly cheap fox and pheasant hunt themes, hung crooked around the room. To the left was the dining room, small and uncomfortable. To the right a small check in counter. Straight ahead was a wide mahogany stair in stark contrast to the pine rimming the rest of the room.

Ian walked over to the counter, Ben following mutely. A pasty-faced man with thinning hair looked up from his Sun. "Yes?"

"I've a reservation," Ian said. "Name's Thorne."

The man coughed, flipped through a thick, musty ledger, a finger scrolling down the list. "Ah, here it is." He produced a key. "Room 11, top of the stairs, to the right. That'll be half up front." The clerk's face had a strange waxy sheen, flecked with silver and green.

Ian paid the man and ushered Ben up the stairs. He inserted the key, opened the door and stepped through. Like the lobby and exterior nothing appeared to have changed in the last few years.

The room was small but bright and cheery. The walls were painted a pale sea-foam green, a leafy, dark green border paper edging the top. There was a desk and a dresser made of oak with a dark, glossy finish. A plain window looked out to the beach and the sea. A double bed sat against the far wall and tucked into the corner was a smaller bed, a child's bed.

Ian went over to the window. The rain had stopped. Below him, the beach spread out along the coast, a grey finger of sand running for as far as the eye could see. The sea was less than calm, grey-green waves rolling and cresting, throwing whitecaps and spray into the dusky air. He recalled walking on the beach, Emily frolicking in the water just out of reach. She loved the water. Ian looked to his left, further down the beach. There, about two-hundred feet from the shoreline, a rock jutted from the sea. It was more a small, rocky, fist-shaped island. Emily would often swim out there, perch herself on the highest point to sun herself, and wait for Ian.

Ian lifted the sash, breathed deeply. The briny sea air tingled his nostrils, and a smile creased Ian's face for the first time in a long while. The water made a sad lap-lapping sound that made him think of children crying. Ian craned his neck, peered out, eyes searching, searching. . . .

Ian turned to Ben. The boy was sitting on the edge of his bed, idly kicking his legs. "Fancy a walk, Ben?"

The boy shrugged.

"We'll put our stuff away later," Ian said. "Let's hit the beach."

Ian grabbed the boy by the hand, hauled him off the bed, out the door, down the stairs and onto the beach. Ben said nothing. He let go of the boy's hand and studied the sea. It was beautiful. He felt a strange attraction to it. The surging waves, the crisp, salt air, the dark, mysterious depths all beckoned him. The sea seemed a sad, strange, lonely place, and that appealed to him.

Ian tottered down to the sea's edge, his sneakered feet sinking into the cool, wet sand. He pulled off his sneakers, rolled up his trousers and waded knee-deep into the cold, cold water. His teeth chattered.

"Come, Ben!" Ian beckoned.

Ben was still, quiet, blank-faced.

"Suit yourself, my boy," Ian said, wading out a bit farther, feeling the strong currents tug at him; liquid tendrils that pulled insistently.

After a while he stepped out of the water.

Ian walked along the beach edge. Ben followed, tiny feet making bird-like impressions in the sand. It was a dreary, dim day. The sea, the sand and the sky were the colour of dead moths. The air was heavy, close, salt-laden.

Ian patted Ben's head. "It's beautiful, isn't it, Ben?"

Ben looked at Ian but said nothing. Ian watched a gull wheel and shriek in the sky and fly out over the grey waves. Something flashed silver on the far horizon. Ian's heart skipped a beat. He pointed.

"Did you see that, Ben?"

Ben gazed with empty eyes.

"What do you think, my boy?" Ian said. "Bird? Fish? Boat?"

Ben shrugged.

Another brief, brilliant glint danced and disappeared. Ian stared, eyes fixed, waiting, waiting, but nothing on the distant horizon came into view. Water lapped at his feet. He glanced down. The tide was pink and red, as if the sea had given birth. A dead fish, cold eye staring, washed up on shore. Pebble-sized eggs, like a string of pearls, trailed from its mouth. The eggs split and tiny iridescent half-fish swam out to sea. Ian imagined they had arms.

The light was fading. Darkness gathered over the sea. Sighing, Ian turned to Ben, lead him back toward their lodgings. Briefly, a sound like children weeping came to him. The sad song of the sea.

෴

Ian woke to the sun spilling warm rays through the window. It was going to be a pleasant day. He sat up, stretched, scratched his head. He went to wake Ben, but discovered the bed empty.

Probably in the loo, Ian thought. He went and rapped on the door.

"Ben? Ben? You in there, Ben?"

When no answer came, he twisted the knob and pushed the door open. The tiny bathroom was empty.

Heart thudding, Ian ran to the window. He threw up the sash and leaned out, scanning the shoreline. Ian sighed. Ben was on the beach, staring out at the calm wine-dark sea.

Ian dressed and went down to the shoreline. He wrapped an arm around the boy's shoulders.

Ben looked up, eyes red and puffy. "Mum?"

Ian hugged him close. "No, son. No."

෴

After a late breakfast, they drove down the road to a nearby maritime museum. The curator, a thin older gentleman with that same waxy silver sheen, was pleased to see them.

"Welcome," he said, in a wet, rattling voice. "Welcome. We don't get many visitors this time of year."

Ian smiled. Ben stared. The curator lead them through the

145

various displays, talking at length about the region's historical port area. As the afternoon wore on, Ian noticed the man's skin become sallow and dry. It lost some of its shine. His eyes appeared to dull, to change shape and colour. Ian was reminded of the dead fish floating on the shoreline.

"Sir?" Ian inquired. "Are you all right?"

"Yes, yes." The man smiled, thin lips pulling back to reveal tiny pointy teeth. "Of course. It's feeding time, is all." He gestured toward the rear of the room. "The two of you must also be in need of sustenance. Would you care to join me? I'd be more than pleased for the company."

Ian nodded. "Sure."

They went through a rear door into the man's small living quarters. It was one room, with a cot and a kitchen, and smelled of fish and seaweed.

"I hope you like fish," the man said, grinning. "It's all I have."

Before Ian could answer the man he was busy filleting and frying fish, his hands a blur of motion. Done, he placed a plate of pan-fried fish in front of Ian and Ben. At his place setting the man placed a grey bucket.

The man reached into the bucket, plucked out a small wriggling silver fish and threw it into his mouth.

"Go ahead, my friends," the man said, pointing at their plates. "Dig in." He grabbed another fish from the bucket, downed it in a gulp. "I hope you don't mind. Young herring. I prefer them this way."

Ian shrugged his shoulders. "Suit yourself."

Ben poked at his food.

"So," the man said, between mouthfuls of herring, "you're looking for something or someone."

Ian dropped his fork. "Huh?"

The man smiled his not unfriendly razor smile. "It's the sea. It draws all kinds, mostly those that are lost or lonely. Like myself."

"Just a vacation," Ian said.

"But you'll find it, friend," the man continued. "You'll find it when you hear its sad refrain." He looked to Ben. "When children weep."

146

Ian stood, forced a smile. "We must be going. Thank you." He shook the man's hand. It was cool and clammy.

The man's mouth puckered, his face shone silver again. "Yes, yes. Of course. My pleasure. I do understand. I'm always here, beholden to the sea, to guide the others."

ଔୟଡ଼

It was late by the time they got back. Ian put Ben to bed then sat beside the window. Like a sea of dancing diamonds, the dark water rippled brilliantly under pale moonlight. It rolled up the shore, silvery-pink waves washing and swallowing the earth.

Ian lifted the sash, breathed in the salt and seaweed. A gleam of white light flared, caught his eye. He watched, waited.

Presently, a fragment of song reached him.

Oh, sad Sargasso. . .
. . .when children weep.

Another silver flame sparked, glinted off the moonlit rock. Ian's heart beat faster. He ran to the bed, shook Ben.

"Come, son, come. To the sea."

Ian pulled the dazed boy from bed, dashed down the stairs and onto the quiet beach. They ran to the shore. Ian peered out at the jutting rock. Moon glow dappled its surface.

A shimmer of silver light flickered, died, flickered again like a light winking on and off. A forlorn wail wafted on the night's cool currents. Ian listened. It died. Then the song came to him in a winsome, haunting hush.

Oh, sad Sargasso, the liquid jewel
Dingy depths summon 'neath
Piscine maidens of fleshless spirit
Who come home when children weep.

Ian smiled, disrobed, stood naked in the pale moonlight. His skin was smooth and green and glossy. He looked at the boy, standing

147

wide-eyed and mute. What, Ian thought, was a boy without his mother?

Nothing.

Ian slid into the water, swam with liquid grace toward the rock. His arms and legs cut easily through the choppy waves, as if he were meant for the sea. Heart hammering, a blood roar in his ears, Ian stopped a few feet away from the rock. He looked up, grinned, waved.

She smiled, slapped her tail on the rock and slipped into the sea, silver scales flashing.

On shore, Ben took a tentative step into the frothy crimson tide.

"Mum?" Ben said.

Ben tottered forward, stopped.

"Mum?"

Weeping, Ben took another step.

Then another.

THE SMELL OF CHAOS IS WRITTEN IN ITS HUES

---

*The attitude that nature is chaotic and
that the artist puts order into it is a
very absurd point of view, I think. All
that we can hope for is to put some
order into ourselves.*
　　　　— Willem de Kooning

You never got to kiss her.

CRSO

K.J. Carter: A Remembrance
by J. Henton
Staff Writer, The Star-Ledger

Perhaps, like the tiny dirigibles that haunt his paintings, K.J. Carter doesn't want to be found.

In certain circles there are theories that artists are born, not made. The same theory holds true for any creative endeavor whether it be writer, photographer, musician, etc. You are either born with the innate ability to create art, or you aren't. Simple, really. Art is not something that can be learned.

I am neither critic nor artist. I can't speak to the relative arguments regarding said theories. I do know that K.J. Carter wasn't born an artist. His was a learned talent, to be sure. There is some talk, though no real evidence, that a young Carter dabbled in the arts. But, lacking any real proof, I would suggest that Carter experimented with drawing and sketching as we all did in our impressionable youth. No more, no less. A brief and passing fascination. It is clear that Carter's burgeoning art career rooted and blossomed in the last two decades.

Only in the recent post 9/11 years has Carter's artwork attracted any critical attention. K.J. Carter's work, oil on masonite, isn't particularly deft. He paints in broad arcing strokes. Not surprising seeing as how Carter's hands are useless lumps of charred flesh, the fingers bent and twisted and fused together. So Carter paints with a brush clamped between his thin, rigid lips.

His paintings are raw and visceral, often angry, and surprisingly melancholy. There's a certain, sad sensitivity underlying the agitated brushstrokes. Carter's world is bleak and heartbreaking. One gets the sense that even if Carter had the use of his hands he'd still paint in wide sweeping strokes, preferring the thick colorful shades that add contrast to his work, rather than a more detailed, less emotional approach. He's no Jackson Pollack or Francis Bacon. No Roy Lichtenstein. But he is K.J. Carter. That will have to be enough.

Then, of course, there are the intangibles – gimmicks, say the critics – that first brought Carter's work to public notice: the smells, yes, *smells*, which seem to emanate from his work.

And the dirigibles.

〇 ぞ〇

On May 6, 1937, your heart burst into flame. It flared brightly, briefly, a white-hot pain burning through your chest, then receding, leaving nothing but ashes and a small dark lump of a heart that would crumble at the slightest provocation. A few hours later, at 7:25 pm in Lakehurst, New Jersey, the Hindenburg, the great German airship, burst into flame and crashed to earth, killing 35. Later, you remember seeing a picture of the Hindenburg, engulfed in fiery flame, broken in the middle so that it resembles a large V. Or a heart. A flaming, broken heart. Still later you saw the newsreels and watched as the giant heart-like dirigible crashed to the ground as if in slow-motion.

35 dead.

Many of the onlookers that day mentioned a smell in the air. A storm was brewing, they said. The sky turned pewter-grey, then green; dark clouds scudded, gathering over Lakehurst like bloated vultures. The air crackled with electricity, and the wind carried a chaotic mixture of scents: ash, oil, gas, and blood. And later, different smells. Singed hair. Burnt flesh. Shattered dreams. Broken hearts.

In Beachwood, New Jersey, southeast of Lakehurst, you sat in the bleachers near the football field, waiting for your girlfriend, Julie, to meet you after school. She'd sidled up to you in the hallway at lunchtime, her face screwed into a gravely serious expression, asking you to meet her, that she has to talk to you, tell you something important. So you sat expectantly on the worn wooden bench, your heart trip-hammering in your chest. You could smell fear and chaos in the air, brought by a cool southerly wind.

You didn't die that day – it only felt like you had.

You were 15 at the time, a grade ten student at Beachwood High. Three hours before the Hindenburg exploded, Julie Stayner—the love of your life, your girlfriend of three and a half weeks, the freckle-faced girl with the full red lips, the girl you sketched in secret before you were going out together, the girl of your dreams— broke up with you. There was someone else, she said. Mark. He was 17. His dad had a car, and a radio. Mark was on the football team. Mark was handsome, sweet. He was *mature*.

Then Julie was gone, rising from the school bleachers to catch up with handsome Mark, who was waving from across the field.

You went home to your bedroom, buried your head in a pillow and wept. And when the great German airship came down to earth, you wept some more.

You never got to kiss her.

⊂℞℈⊃

Carter's most famous—some say infamous—piece of art hangs in the gallery in New York's Port Authority building. The piece, "The Smell of Chaos is Written in its Hues", like all the pieces in the Port Authority gallery, deals directly with the harrowing events of 9/11. And, like all of K.J. Carter's efforts, this piece is crude but emotionally effective. This particular painting measures 3 feet by 4 feet (one of the larger pieces Carter has painted) and is, like every other K.J. Carter piece, oil on masonite. He preferred, obviously, rigid masonite over pliable canvas.

What differentiates this work from other Carter paintings is the perspective, the point of view. Instead of your stock, straight-on view, Carter dropped his vision down. Imagine a camera in the middle of the road, on the hard ground, viewfinder slightly raised, a wide-angle lens capturing the events. Carter's painting, a kaleidoscope of grays and greens, captures a scene mere moments after Tower 1 collapsed. People are running. They are daubed in browns and grays. Art critics suggest that Carter is devaluing them, rendering them less than ordinary, a comment on the general nature of terrorism. Gray people. To me there is a simpler explanation; they are covered in dust. You've no doubt seen the news footage, and the photos. New York City, on that day, was a nuclear winter.

Because of the low angle of the painting I notice their feet and legs first, in mid-step, trying to get away. Then my eyes pan up to see their faces frozen in wretched terror; eyes wide, mouths screaming. Behind them, like some terrible demon coughed from the very pits of hell, a roiling green cloud of dust, dirt, and debris rolls down the street, chasing after them. Behind and above the cloud, in the sky, is stark green-grey emptiness. Somehow, that empty space is infinitely more terrifying than anything else in the painting. It is a big hole punched through the heart.

Standing in the gallery, staring at the bold lines and dizzying whorls, is a heady experience. Though done in somewhat muted hues, the painting seems alive. The people, caught in a terrible stasis, are about to be engulfed by the advancing dust devil.

I can smell the terror, the chaos. Literally. Carter's work, whether the Pine Barrens in New Jersey or a corn field in Iowa, gives off strangely unpleasant odors. The corn field smells of butter. The Pine Barrens smell of rotted leaves. And his 9/11 piece is a pungent assortment of briny sweat, metallic blood, and the acid tang of fear.

It is uncertain how Carter achieves this effect. A special treatment or additive, perhaps, added to his paints, or sprayed on later like a fine lacquer. No one knows for certain. We do know that a K.J. Carter work attacks the senses. Not only can I see and smell the scene, but I imagine I can hear and taste it, as well. I have to resist the urge to reach out and touch each painting.

CR&SO

In the following weeks, with your paper-thin heart thumping hollowly in your chest, you repeatedly watched the newsreels of the mighty Zeppelin crashing to earth like some modern day Goliath. Wide-eyed, you studied the pictures published in the Star-Ledger. You spent many hours at The Beachwood Public Library, reading up on Count Ferdinand von Zeppelin. You began to sketch your own Zeppelins, in pencils and charcoals and ink, and tacked them up on your bedroom walls beside the sketches of Julie that still dotted your room. And each sketch, each drawing, hurt you to the core, stabbed you in the heart. It brought back that day, May 6, in all its ignoble glory. You could, in your mind's eye, see it.

You could *smell* it.

CR&SO

Why dirigibles? And why are they half-hidden, almost ambiguous, amorphous blobs? One wonders if Carter had meant for them to be seen. And yet, if I study any Carter piece long enough I'll see the zeppelin blended into a street scene or mountain; merged with a cloud or highway; inserted into the flames of a church fire or plunged into the murky waters of a city river. Never large, the dirigibles, but always present. It is Carter's calling card, his signature.

It got to be a game, though. Spot the dirigible. And it detracts from the Carter oeuvre. For Carter is a genuine talent. His body of work contains a number of stunning pieces. Art that hits you in the gut. Whether you like his work or not, there's no denying that it leaves a lasting impression. One hopes that Carter will continue to thrill us with his work.

One hopes that Carter will be found.

☙❧

You saw *her* everywhere: at school; in the park; at the Library; at the soda shop. You couldn't get away from her. And it hurt. Lord, how it hurt. So you skipped class, feigned illness, stayed in your room. And still it hurt. Because you couldn't get her out of your head, couldn't stop thinking of her. Thinking of the curve of her neck and the sparkle of her eyes. Thinking about the way her hair shone like golden honey in the sun, the way it moved when she flipped it over a shoulder. And you couldn't stop thinking about the way she smelled; Autumn rain and a field of lavender.

So, alone in your room you sketched, as tears leaked from your eyes and ran down your cheeks. And you plastered all the walls, every available inch, with images of the Zeppelin, and, though it pained you greatly, you tacked up pictures of Julie. If you studied the drawings, really studied them, you could smell them. The Zeppelins smelled of dread and panic. Julie smelled of cool peppermint rain and sweet lilac. You would lie in your bed, the sharp scents intermingling, dreaming and thinking. Dreaming and thinking.

When there was no room left on your walls you decided to build your own Zeppelin, a miniature version of the great airship. So you gathered some material; wood and rubber, nails and glue. And you

154

fashioned a crude likeness of the blimp and you hung it from the ceiling. You watched it twirl in a phantom breeze as you cried yourself to sleep.

CRSO

I've followed Carter's career for a number of years. He's a local boy. I first saw one of his pieces in a tiny gallery in Cherry Hill. I did some digging, and came across more of his paintings in small galleries in even smaller towns. I was struck immediately by the vibrancy in his work. And the pain. Here was an unflinching artist who painted from the heart, with passion and verve. I was effusive in my praise for his work. I still am.

With the help of a local arts patron, I tracked Carter down. I wanted an interview. Carter had never really consented to any interview requests from the media. He was a solitary figure. A recluse, if you will. He was content to sell a few paintings, and get his commission. Frankly, he didn't seem to want the attention. The art world wanted to know how he did it, how he managed to infuse his painting with appropriate scents. They wanted to know the secret of the dirigibles.

And I wanted to know those things, as well.

CRSO

One day you'd had enough. You woke, your heart silent, cold, a dead thing. Slowly, standing in the middle of your too small room, a rage built up in you. You leaped at the walls like a wild thing, clawing at the sketches, pulling them down and shredding them, every last one of them. The floor and bed and dressers were piled high with torn bits and scraps of paper. And you slumped to the ground, amid the papery ruins, exhausted. Staring up at the ceiling, your breath huffing in your chest, you noticed the Zeppelin, spinning, spinning....

And you had an idea.

Standing, you pulled the Zeppelin from the ceiling. You scooped a handful of paper from the floor and placed it on the bottom of your small, metal trashcan. You put the Zeppelin into the trashcan. Carrying the trashcan, you went down the hallway, into your father's study, took the Zippo lighter from his desk, and hurried out to the back patio.

CRSO

Through guile, and a bit of deception, I got K.J. Carter's phone number from a New Jersey area art dealer. I called him up and requested an interview. He laughed humorlessly and hung up. So I called again, and before he could hang up, I asked if he'd let me see him work. I would ask no questions, I told him. I just wanted to observe. There was a long silence. I thought he'd not heard me. But then he grunted an affirmative, and grudgingly gave me his address.

Carter now lived near Lakehurst, the site of the Hindenburg disaster. The Zeppelin connection now seemed patently obvious. But my records showed he'd grown up in Beachwood, and had only recently moved to Lakehurst.

It was a warm August day when I went out to see K.J. Carter. Cicadas sang. The pavement rippled. And a slight breeze stirred the ancient willows. Carter lived (and presumably still does, if he can be found) in a small bungalow in the country. The house was quaint, if a little unloved.

Silently, without fanfare, Carter opened the door and ushered me in. He was pale, thin, unshaven, and his hooded eyes shone with a dark mystery. There was brusqueness in his manner. He pointed into the next room, gesturing for me to precede him, and I caught a good glimpse of his hands. They were small bright pink things, the size and colour of newborn birds. The fingers were bent and tangled like the roots of a tree.

I followed Carter into the next room, his studio. The far wall held an enormous window that looked out upon a wide, deep yard that was in need of mowing. A stark, dead Oak stood in the middle of the grass like some alien sentinel, one thick skeletal branch reaching to the sky like an outstretched arm. All told, Carter had a couple acres of prime New Jersey land. I began to speak, eager to say something, but Carter shushed me like a parent would a troublesome toddler. He nodded, indicating a stool, and I sat.

Carter shuffled over to a large easel holding a generous piece of clean brown masonite, and sat. He leaned over, and using his mouth, pulled a moist brush from a cup on the easel's tray. K.J. Carter bent to his paints and began to create.

For the next few hours I sat, quietly entranced, as Carter painted. His head and brush whipped about in a frenetic blur, filling in huge swaths with a few rudimentary strokes. Sweat poured from him. Often he'd stand, kicking the stool away, and sway in front of the painting, as if dancing, his brush cutting deep lines through the thick globules of paint. Then he'd sit again, seemingly doing detail work, his head and body jerking spastically. On occasion, Carter would stop, catch his breath and have a sip of water from a nearby pitcher. The respite would be momentary, though, and Carter would again attack the easel, pouring every ounce of pain and passion and pride into the work.

Eventually, more than three hours after he'd first started, Carter lost all his energy and he slumped on his stool, deflated. The brush fell limply from his lips. He was done.

I went and stared at the finished work. And smiled. Ochre and pale purples. It wasn't hard to find the dirigible. It sat in the middle of a violet sky, dominating the painting. A field of tall blond grass spread beneath the airship, waving. A lone tree with a reaching branch anchored the left side of the painting. A yellow spotlight shone from the undercarriage of the Zeppelin, highlighting a lone figure, (Carter, I knew) in the middle of the field. Carter's head was upraised, and one hand, perfect and unmarred, was raised in a wave or subtle entreaty. And the painting carried a delicate scent of lilac with a hint of rain. Here, obviously, was Carter's most intimate and personal piece of art. I stood gaping at the piece, and slowly, in the curve of the Zeppelin, melded perfectly with the tones and lines, I saw a face. It was a young girl, not yet a woman, smiling, freckle-faced, her hair waving like the tall grass below her. I looked to Carter, the real flesh and blood Carter sitting beside me. A wide smile creased his face. His eyes were moist.

157

"Why?" I asked, though I wasn't supposed to ask anything.

Faintly, barely more than a whisper, he answered. "I never got to kiss her."

⊗⊗

You placed the trashcan on the patio stones. The nose of the Zeppelin poked out of the end as if it were trying to lift off, trying to escape. You reached into the can, thumbed the wheel of the lighter, and held it to the paper lining the bottom. In seconds it was alight. You watched as the flames spread, as they engulfed the Zeppelin. You watched as the miniature airship burnt and crumbled, folding in on itself, just like your heart did. You lifted your hands, clenched your fingers into claws. You wouldn't sketch again, ever, so you plunged them into the fire. And held them there. And it hurt, almost as much as it did that day in May. And the smell, the smell…. But still you held your hands in the fire.

⊗⊗

If K.J. Carter isn't found, if he doesn't return, we are poorer for his absence. He was a visionary artist. His work will be discussed and dissected, and more importantly, enjoyed, for years to come. I hate speaking about him in the past tense, but I believe we've seen the last of K.J. Carter. We've seen the last of any new, original Carter art. His last piece, "Prelude to a Kiss", which he painted in his studio that August day, was his swan song. Though there is a certain sad finality to the piece, I felt that Carter himself was upbeat, hopeful, and happy. At the end of the day he seemed a changed man from the one who first opened his door to me. He seemed a man unburdened.

So I wasn't surprised a week later, acting on a hunch, when I went out to visit Carter and he wasn't there. His front door was locked, so I went around to the back. The door from his studio, which led to the backyard, was wide open. I walked into the studio, calling his name, knowing in my heart of hearts that Carter wasn't there. That he would never again grace this house, this studio.

Stepping back out to the yard, I was struck by the smell of lilacs. I smiled, closed Carter's back door, and went home.

K.J. Carter, I knew, wasn't coming back. He'd found whatever it was he was looking for.

CRSO

You never married. You never *dated*. You floated through college and into your thirties and forties not thinking, not dreaming. It was easier that way. You held a number of menial, unimportant jobs, never letting your co-workers get too close, never trusting anyone but yourself. Then, in your fifties, when most people are contemplating retirement, winding their lives down, you began to think of *her*. And it still hurt, just a bit, but you found that it was good thing. You found it made you feel alive. Found it was better than not thinking, not feeling.

So you began to paint, pouring all those lonely, wasted years, all your blood, sweat and tears, into your work. And it felt good. And you were happy.

You painted for years and years, and sold some pieces, and made some money. Your work was reviled and praised. You didn't care. You painted for you, not them.

You painted for *her*.

Then, one day, you realized you'd accomplished all you could. You were done. Finished. You had, in your later years, made a contribution. And you were happy, really happy.

So one fine August day you stepped into your backyard, as if beckoned. A golden light shone in your eyes but you were not blinded. You took a step. Then another. And another.

And you didn't look back.

WOLVES AND ANGELS

Wolves, the old woman had said. *The wolves are at the door.*

Bryn grimaces, remembering mother's clear, strong voice. It was as if she were in the same room with the woman, not hundreds of miles away over a phone line. There was a peculiar tone to mother's voice. Resignation? Hope?

The car winds its way through the icy, back country roads, wheels spinning and the car sliding around every bend. The heater in the car is failing. The radiator is leaking, and Bryn, panicked and rushing from Mother's sudden phone call, had forgotten to add the anti-freeze to the rusty radiator. So the windows are icing over, little filaments of frost creeping in on the edges.

Since her father's death, Bryn has felt dark shadows slinking around at the edges of her vision, invading her life, skulking ice-like at the corners of her eyes. It was like viewing the world through a camera obscura, a dim vignette. Now, with her mother slipping into senility, the dark shadows crowded her life.

She sprays windshield washer fluid on the windows and lets the wipers clear away some of the slush and ice. But the ice creeps back, blurring her vision, making an already treacherous drive all the more dangerous.

Bryn hates this road. Hates her mother now for making her drive it again.

As a child, in summertime, Bryn and her parents would take this winding road into their cottage. The road twists its way through thick stands of pine and birch; through massive rock cuts that jut out like an angry fist. Traveling through the dark pine forest, Bryn always imagined golden eyes staring at her with intense curiosity. It

161

made her shiver and cringe in the backseat of the car. Her young mind dreamt of all the things that could happen to her if she were lost in the forest.

Mostly Bryn hates this road because it meant leaving the city behind for the summer. It was just her and her parents in the tiny wooden cottage. No television, no indoor plumbing; and millions of spiders and mosquitoes. Every time she went outside, shadows lurked nearby, watching her. She heard branches snapping, birds shrieking, and the heavy crunch of some forest beast lumbering through the pines. So she'd sit in the cottage, reading, and playing board games or cards, the smell of pine a cloying, oppressive entity hanging in the air.

Rounding a bend in the road, a dark shape darts in front of the car. Bryn hits the brake pedal, cranks the steering wheel to the right. The car swerves past the fleeting shadow and slides onto the narrow shoulder, then into the shallow ditch. Bryn curses, punches the steering wheel. Glancing up she sees the dark shape moving among the thick pines. A deer, she thinks. There are lots of deer in eastern Ontario.

She steps from the vehicle, walks around to the front. The ditch is wide but shallow. The front bumper leans into the narrow rut. Aside from the neon green trail of fluid leaking into the snow, it doesn't look too bad. Shaking, she pulls her cigarettes from the purse in the car and smokes one while leaning on the vehicle's hood. Bryn gets back into the car, starts the engine, puts it into reverse, and hits the gas. The tires spin. The tang of burning metal stung her nose. She shifts the car into a lower gear and gently presses down on the accelerator. For a brief moment the tires spin uselessly, then they catch and the car backs up onto the road. The engine makes a strange coughing noise. Bryn straightens the car and continues on her way. It isn't far now.

CR8O

She stands in the doorway of the bedroom, stares at the frail, old woman; the stranger; her mother. The room is hot and smells like piss.

She's dying.

Bryn blinks. Something in her chest slowly shifts, and she wonders if it is her heart. Last month, and the month before, Bryn made the drive out to the cottage. She witnessed her mother slowly wither and fade like an ancient oak long past its prime. Saw her eyes grow dull, her skin pale and sag. Soon, Bryn thinks, she'll be nothing so much as a cracked leaf blowing in a chill autumn wind; breaking up, dissolving, scattering like ashes.

The old woman's eyelids flutter like butterfly wings and open. Her cloudy, milk-white gaze roams the small, stuffy room, and come to rest on Bryn.

"Hello?" croaks the old woman. She raises a palsied, shaking hand; points at Bryn. "Who's this?"

Bryn steps into the bedroom, sighs. "It's me, mother. Bryn. Your daughter."

The old woman's face crinkles in confusion. "Oh," she says. "Oh. Yes, now I remember you. You're my daughter. I thought you were dead."

Bryn moves to the side of the bed. "You called, mother. I'm here." Bryn sees a large, wide, ceramic bowl on the floor, filled with urine. She blanches. "Dear, God, mother. Why didn't you call me sooner?"

Her mother sits up, stares at Bryn with small dry eyes. "Ah, it's you, Bryn. I never thought I'd see you again."

Bryn flinches. "I'm your daughter."

"Family," the old woman whispers. "Me, you... and your father." The old woman turns her head, looks out the window. "He's just taken the boat out. James loves the lake. It's a fine day, isn't it?" She grabs hold of Bryn's arm, squeezes, looks up at Bryn like a child asking for a treat. "He'll be back soon." It's more a question than a statement.

James! Her father. When her father retired, Bryn's parents poured their savings into the cottage; adding rooms, plumbing, and electricity. They sold their city home and moved into the cottage. They loved the country life. By that time Bryn was away at university and rarely visited the old homestead, no matter the many modern amenities. Besides, she reasoned, her parents deserved their time together.

But then father became gravely ill, his mind and spirit slipping away like smoke on a summer breeze. More and more frequently he'd appear confused, forgetful. Dementia began to grip him. And one summer morning at the cottage he wrote a long note – a love letter – to Bryn's mother, left it on the table beside a vase of fresh-picked country lilies and a faded photo of the two of them during their courtship, and took the rowboat out into the lake and slipped quietly into the cool waters. His body was never recovered. In her mind's eye, she sees a misty morning, an empty rowboat, and small ripples spreading out on the glassy lake surface.

Bryn blinks, shakes the memory from her thoughts.

She shakes off her mother's fierce grip, pulls a ratty orange afghan up to her chin, tucks it in. "Can I get you anything, mother?"

The old woman considers for a very long time. "No," she says, finally. "I'm going to rest now, dear."

Bryn tries a smile. "That's a good idea. I'm here now. I'll check in on you. It'll be alright."

"Tell me, dear," the old woman asks, "did you see them?"

"See what, mother?"

"The wolves?"

Bryn snorts. "You're dreaming, mother."

"Yes, I suppose I am." The old woman closes her eyes, but continues to speak. "They hunger, Bryn. Do you? Do you hunger for anything?"

Bryn lets out a heavy breath, lifts the urine-filled bowl and leaves the room.

☙❧

Standing on the outside deck, Bryn shivers. It's snowing. Fat flakes cascading from a pearly sky. Despite her parka, the cold leaks into her. She trembles, stamps her feet like a nervous stallion. Bryn

164

fishes a cigarette pack from the coat pocket, shakes one out, lights it, inhales deeply and blows out a stream of blue smoke. She watches the smoke catch on the chill wind and dissolve like so many things in her life.

The cottage is built high on a promontory, overlooking the small finger lake below. With the gentle snow falling, Bryn admits it is a beautiful view. The pines to the left and right are limned in frost, glowing with spectral light; the lake is a sheet of sparkling glass dusted with snow. She feels as if she's caught in a snow-globe; shaken and disoriented. Bryn recalls sitting on this deck in summertime, sipping Coke, watching the magenta sunsets and the neon fireflies, swatting black flies. She smiles. *Such simple beauty,* she thinks. *Why didn't I see it?* She wonders how she could stay so long in Toronto, the grey city, in her grey work cubicle, wearing her grey clothes.

The words reverberate in Bryn's head. *I thought you were dead.*

Bryn stamps out the cigarette, goes down the deck stairs, and across the yard to the edge of the lake. She takes a tentative step, then another. Frozen solid. She doesn't hear any cracking. Bryn moves carefully along the ice, skating on booted feet. She kneels down, bends and draws a stick figure in the snow. Then she draws a big happy face. A smiley. Inspired, Bryn lies down on the ice face-up, staring at the wide canvas of sky. Soft snow falls steadily from the vast pewter expanse. She opens her mouth, sticks out her tongue, tries to catch the flakes. Then she presses her arms and legs tight to the cold ground and moves them along the ice in sweeping motions. A snow angel! Bryn hasn't made a snow angel in a very long time. She stands, examines the angel. Smiles. You can't make snow angels in the city, she thinks. And Bryn realizes she hasn't been outside all winter. Day after grey day, she walks from her apartment to the subway to the office building. And on the weekends she shops, and reads, and runs errands. All inside. She hasn't been outside, living. Bryn wonders when her mother last ventured outside.

As a child, Bryn wanted to be the next great figure skating champion. The next Dorothy Hamill. With her short wedge of a haircut, she even looked a little like Dorothy Hamill. Standing on the lake ice, Bryn imagines she's a young Dorothy. In her heavy boots, she skates out further on the lake. Bryn spins, jumps. She skates along in great sweeping arcs. She twirls, falls to her knees, throws kisses to her adoring fans. For once she's the drama queen, the center of attention. Laughing, panting, Bryn lies down on the thin webbing of snow. She catches her breath, then makes another snow angel, moving her arms and legs until the ice is smooth and polished. Gleaming mirror-bone.

Bryn rises, shakes the wet snow from her arms. From this vantage, the cottage is a small dark stone, ringed in stands of pine and birch; their skeletal branches like fingers reaching. Turning, she inspects her snow angel. It's a bright, shining, symmetrical jewel. In the fold of one wing, something catches Bryn's eye. A sliver of movement under the murky ice. She kneels, brushes the spot on the ice, leans close and sees a slim pale hand.

Bryn gasps, pedals backwards along the ice like a drunken crab. It can't be, she thinks. Scrambling to her knees, Bryn crawls slowly forward, peers at the ice. And there's the pale hand, the arm trailing into the darkness. The hand is at rest, lying dormant in the thick ice. Bryn is reminded of Michelangelo's *Creation of Adam*, how Adam's arm, though touched by God, is held in such casual repose. Heart racing, she rubs her eyes, blinks. And the hand is gone. Under the ice, something stirs. Bryn leans close. A wan pale face swims up to view. Bryn pales, trembles. She's stricken; frozen in stasis. Father! There's a half-smile on his face. His eyes are closed. Relaxed. Content. He's an angel, Bryn thinks. She reaches out, touches the ice, rubs a gloved a hand over the smooth surface in a tender caress. When she lifts her hand, there is nothing there but gleaming ice and wet snow. No hand. No face of an angel. Bryn spreads her arms, falls to the ice, rests her cheek on the cool, cool surface, and closes her eyes. She thinks she can stay here for a very long time.

ः ॐ ॐ

Looking down at her mother, Bryn can't see any movement. No chest heaving, or facial tics or stirring. Alarmed, she gently shakes the old woman, whispers. "Mother?"

The old woman stirs, opens her sleep-encrusted eyes. "James?"

Bryn breathes a sigh of relief. "No, mother, it's me, Bryn."

"Ah, Bryn, you're back." The old woman smiles warmly. "It's good to see you. I was having the most wonderful dream. There were angels. Beautiful angels. And wolves. They were at the door. I was going to let them in." The old woman glances at the frost-covered window. "Did you see your father?"

"Yes," Bryn whispers. "Yes. I did." And she doesn't know why, but she lies. "He'll be along shortly, mother."

"It won't be much longer," the old woman says.

Bryn pulls the dresser chair up to the side of the bed and sits. She takes her mother's hand in her own. So small, she thinks. Skin and bones.

The old woman coughs, blinks. "Bryn? Is that you?"

"Yes, it's me." She strokes her mother's hand. A tear wells up and slips from Bryn's eye. "It'll be all right."

"You'll take me to see him?"

"What?"

The old woman stares in earnest at Bryn. "James. Your father. I'll see him again?"

And Bryn lies again. "Yes, of course. I promise."

With some effort and help from Bryn, her mother sits up. "Did you see the pack?" Bryn's mother asks.

Bryn shakes her head. "The what?"

"The wolf pack."

Wolves, her mother had said. *The wolves are at the door.*

"No," Bryn says. "I haven't seen any wolves." But then she recalls a dark shape bounding past her car, and she shivers.

"They're beautiful, dear. Each winter they come across the ice to feed on the deer. There's a family of them. A family." Her mother is grinning, lucid. And Bryn notices the excitement in her voice. Notices the wistful way she lingered on the word "family."

And suddenly Bryn is crying. She sobs, stares at her mother through tear-blurred eyes. "I'm sorry, mother."

"It's okay, dear," the old woman says, stroking Bryn's arm. "You've nothing to be sorry about."

Bryn wipes a hand over her eyes. "I—I should have been around more. I see that now."

"Nonsense. You've your own life to live." The old woman's eyes are shining. "Besides, you're here now. That's all I wanted. To see you. And soon I'll see James."

"Mother—"

The old woman leans forward, her eyes bright and fierce. Cogent. "Shush, now, Bryn. It's all I want. I'm old and tired." Then her face collapses and a sob wracks her body. "It's all I've ever wanted."

Bryn stands, leans over and wraps the afghan tight around her mother's body. Then she scoops her mother up in her arms and carries her out of the bedroom. Her mother weighs hardly anything, and somehow Bryn isn't surprised. There isn't much left of her.

The old woman stares curiously at Bryn. "What are you doing? Where are we going?"

Bryn walks through the living room and pushes through the back door, onto the deck. She places her mother gently in a chair, bundles the afghan tightly around her.

"I want you to see the view, the snow, the lake," Bryn says.

The old woman smiles weakly. "Bryn? Is that you?"

"Yes."

Bryn's mother turns, looks out at the lake. "Oh. I thought… for just a moment… well…."

Bryn follows her mother's gaze. "Yes. I know. He's out there."

The two women sit and watch the swirling eddies of snow. Bryn breathes deeply. The scent of pine prickles her nose. Once, she hated that smell. Today it is as pleasant as the most exquisite perfume. The air is cool, but the light is warm, soft. Bryn thinks that Monet would have been impressed.

Far across the frozen lake, Bryn sees movement, a dark shape on the far horizon.

"They're coming," the old woman says.

And Bryn can see them, the wolves, four of them bounding across the ice, shadowy grey specters in a snow-white world. She watches them approach, moving swiftly across the ice with a loping grace she'd never imagined. They draw nearer, their eyes glinting, breath fogging the air. She wonders about their sharp teeth, their hot breath, their hunger. She can almost feel their single-mindedness, their sense of purpose. For a brief, terrible moment Bryn wants nothing more to do than to dash out onto the ice and run with the wolves.

"Don't take me away," the old woman says. There's a broad child-like grin creasing her mother's face.

"What?" Bryn asks.

"When it's time, I don't want to go. Everything I wanted is here. And I know he's out there." The old woman points toward the lake. "Take me out there."

Bryn is about to protest, but her mother sighs, closes her eyes. Her head lolls to the side. Bryn scoops her up in her arms and carries her inside, places mother on the bed. Her mother's mouth moves silently. She settles into sleep. Bryn sits with her for a while, watches every shallow breath, every twitch and tick and rustle, then moves back outside to the deck.

She waits for the wolves, and near dusk they come out of the forest and start across the lake; the largest wolf, a shaggy silver-grey ghost-wolf, drags a dead deer that leaves a jagged dark trail.

Standing at the deck rail, staring out at the silver and grey world, watching the pack pull the bloody carcass along the lake, Bryn lights a cigarette and tries not to cry. Twilight brings a strange melancholy. Tiny specks of ice float in the air, borne on gentle winds. The air shimmers and glitters as if someone has waved a wand and sprinkled fairy dust. The wolves have disappeared along the far horizon; grey ghosts slipping into a grey netherworld, a dark stain marking their passage. She sits on a deck chair, smoking, shivering, until dusk turns to night, until the world goes from grey to black. She sleeps and dreams of icy angels, her dead father, and hungry wolves.

CR₰

She wakes cold and shaking. A golden sun is shining in a denim sky. The lake is flat and silvery, a tarnished mirror. Clumps of wet snow drop from the pines — the trees sloughing off winter's weight. She moves to the deck rail, lights a cigarette. Gazing down the side of the hill, Bryn sees the thin grey wolf standing where the lake meets the pines. The wolf stares up at her, unmoving, black eyes flashing in the sunshine. Bryn thinks she can see shadowy movement in the trees. She lights another cigarette, watches the wolf watching her. After a long while, with the wolf still staring up at her, Bryn turns and goes into the cottage.

Bryn goes to her mother, gently puts a hand on her face. The face is cold but smiling, the eyes closed, at rest. Peaceful. It reminds Bryn of her father's frozen face. She gathers her mother in her arms, kisses her cheek. Carries her out to the deck. The wolf is gone.

Carrying her mother, Bryn moves down the deck stairs to the side of the house. She moves to her car and places her mother in the passenger seat, fishes out her keys, and slides into the driver's side. Bryn places the key in the ignition, but doesn't turn it. She lights a cigarette, instead. She smokes the cigarette down to the filter, grinds it out in the ashtray. She stares through the foggy windshield at the lake, then looks at her mother. Bryn strokes her mother's arm. She pulls the key from the ignition and pockets it.

Crying, Bryn takes her mother from the passenger seat, carries her down to the bright, frozen lake. She slides out onto the slushy surface, places her mother down. Bryn had wanted to make another snow angel, to show her mother, but the snow has melted. She sits cross-legged on the ice, smokes, stares at the sun, stares at her mother, and wipes the tears from her eyes. Bryn bends, wipes a spot of ice clean, peers into the frozen lake but doesn't see anything. Looking up, she gazes toward the horizon, but again sees nothing. She reaches over, wraps the afghan around her mother's body as tight as she can, then she stands. Bryn turns and walks across the melting lake, toward the shore.

Back in the cottage she makes a cup of instant coffee and carries it out onto the deck. She can see mother on the ice, a bright bundle of orange. Bryn sips her coffee, smokes two cigarettes. Soon, she sees them. The wolves. They move swiftly across the lake, with purpose, and stop at her mother. The pack circles, sniffs, and the Alpha howls. Then their mouths latch onto mother and they drag her away, her passage leaving a wide trail in the slush.

Bryn watches until the dark spots disappear along the horizon, then, with nowhere else to go, she turns and goes into the cottage.

BOULEVARD OF BROKEN DREAMS

(with Scott Thomas)

Lawrence always wanted to be the good guy; the one in the white hat, riding to the rescue.

☙❦❧

It rained. Of course it rained. Lawrence was underdressed, he had no umbrella, and the bus station was no more than a rusty sign and a once-green bench with nothing like a roof above it. And, to make things worse, the bus was late. It was turning out to be one of *those* days.

For a while he held his Telegram over his head, but the rain, drumming, perhaps fingering the printed words as if Braille, soon reduced the newspaper to a flaccid, soggy thing. Lawrence imagined he looked like a drowned nun.

The bus came at last. It was a dreary behemoth of diesel fumes and silver-grey paint, the windows foggy and containing a few bland blurry faces. He looked at the wan faces. *She* wasn't there. But he'd never given up hope. He'd been looking. Looking for a long time. Hoping to see her. Hoping to catch a glimpse of her on a street corner; in a diner; at the park; on a city bus. Lawrence never saw her. And, in his heart of hearts, he knew he never would. They'd found her – at least parts of her, anyway – all those years ago. He felt like he was chasing a smoke ghost. But he wandered the streets, and rode the buses, and never gave up hope.

He always wanted to be the good guy, in the white Stetson, riding to the rescue. But it was too late for that.

Lawrence took up his overnight bag and boarded.

He headed straight for the back of the bus, as if on instinct. He'd always preferred the backs of buses, and the far rows at theaters, the rear seats in classrooms, anything that might, in some vague way, approximate invisibility. Anything that might afford him a better view of his surroundings.

The bus squealed like a rat in a blender, then jerked into motion. The city streets, the buildings, and even the poor bastards rushing along in the rain, seemed to be conjured in rough strokes of graphite. Even passing neon seemed anemic in the downpour.

Lawrence was alone in the back of the bus, his nearest neighbors sitting several rows up. The bus was far from crowded, which he liked, though it smelled damp, infused with the scents of many bodies, each with its own tell-tale odor, be it perfume or sweat or booze.

For a while, as the bus shambled along its route, Lawrence dozed. And he dreamed. As was often the case, he dreamed of Emily. Her pale face swam up to him. Her mouth opened, and she spoke two tiny words. *"To be."*

Lawrence woke with a start. To be? What the hell does that mean? "Or not to be," he said aloud. "That is the question." He shook his head and noticed something from the corner of his eye. There was a limp grey raincoat slumped on the seat beside him. At first he wondered if the owner of the garment was somewhere up front, maybe chatting with an acquaintance, and would return, but after five, then ten minutes, the bus bumping down narrow, grubby city streets, he realized that someone had forgotten the coat, and left it there.

He looked down at the coat. It was slumped on the seat in such a way as to suggest that someone had been wearing it, and had simply dematerialized, sinking into the cracked red leather seat as if it were quick-sand. It was a well-worn item; it had spent time out in harsh weather, and there were stained areas where the grey was darker than the rest. He couldn't tell if it had belonged to a man or a woman.

As the city smeared by the windows, Lawrence debated looking in the pockets. Maybe there was something that would identify the coat's owner. A scrap of paper, or, more unlikely, a wallet. He was not entirely comfortable with this course of action, but he found himself touching it nonetheless.

Lawrence looked up, slightly ashamed, but the passengers, tan and grey blobs, lumps of malleable clay, ignored him as he reached for the coat. He tried the breast pocket first. He didn't care for the feel of the material against his fingers. What if there were terrible germs squatting in the material, ready to pounce on him? He felt something strange—it was hard and slender, but there was softness as well. He pulled the object out and sneered.

It was a rabbit's foot good luck charm, though its appearance did not inspire thoughts of fortuity. It was old, little more than spindly lengths of bone, but for a few clumps of lingering hair like the spores from a dandelion. Lawrence dropped the foot back into the pocket.

The right-hand waist pocket contained no more than a wad of Kleenex. The left-hand pocket held a small piece of amber that had been fashioned to look like a tooth. A translucent honey-colored molar. Lawrence doubted it was a natural formation—it was too perfect to be a fluke, no matter how many centuries of rain and erosion had been at it.

Lawrence put the tooth back and opened the coat. The tails of the thing were spread over his thighs. There was indeed an inside pocket, and there was something in it; he could see a slender band of flat white pocking up. He carefully pinched the edge of whatever was tucked in there and slid it out. He openly gasped when he saw the photograph.

It was Emily, *her*, his sister, starring at him from a yellowed Polaroid, gazing at him through crease-cracks like frozen static. The picture shook in Lawrence's hand. He wagged his head; it couldn't be her. It had to be someone who simply looked like her. They had found her leg bones, hadn't they, after she vanished off an uptown bus twenty years back? A bus he should have been on. She had been eleven years old at the time. Eleven.

Lawrence suddenly remembered that Emily had been carrying her rabbit's foot at the time of her abduction. He remembered pressing it into her tiny palm for good luck. Remembered her pale, smiling face through the bus window as the bus lurched down the street. Remembered a figure in a long grey coat and black cowboy hat sitting behind Emily, turning a blank, featureless face toward him.

Lawrence grimaced. His chest tightened, and his heart felt heavy, like a stone.

Yeah, some good luck charm, he thought.

He began to cry, and the feelings surprised him. It had been twenty years. Twenty years! His body trembled, and tears leaked from the corners of his eyes. He blinked, stared out the dirt-smeared, rain-blurred window at the dirt-smeared, tear-blurred world. The rain had let up. Gray fog hovered above the slick, empty streets, trapping the world in a drear torpor, like a fly in molasses.

Glancing up, Lawrence noticed he was alone. The bus had stopped, front and rear doors standing open expectantly. The passengers, the lumps of clay, had left, leaving mysterious murky little puddles that shimmered suggestively. Even the bus driver had disappeared.

Alone! It was a word, a feeling, he was all too familiar with. He'd felt alone ever since Emily had gone.

Christ, she'd only been eleven years old. Or, as she often reminded him on that long ago summer, eleven and a *half*.

It was a summer of adventure and wonder; magic and mystery. A summer of sunshine. He was thirteen. And things were different back then. You didn't need to lock your door at night. Neighbors spoke to each other, were friendly, held block parties. Every day held the promise of childhood excitement. He'd awake each morning to the bluest of blue skies. A sky the colour of Robin's eggs and wizard's hats and cotton candy. And he and Emily would dash out into the street, skipping breakfast, and play hopscotch or ride

176

their bikes. In the afternoon they'd go to the community pool to swim and lie in the sun, their skin golden and bronze. No one used sunscreen. Later, he and Emily would head to the corner store to buy Pop Rocks and Black Balls, licorice and gum. They'd walk home together, Emily smiling, laughing at his jokes. No one else laughed at his jokes. After supper they'd go to the library to sit in silence in the dark corners to read about Tom Sawyer and Huck Finn and Peter Pan. Some nights they would sneak out and go to the park, sit cross-legged under the bright moon and watch the fireflies, listen to the crickets. They would pluck blades of grass, stretch them into a makeshift reed between their thumbs and blow, making night music; the music of bullfrogs, and owls. The music of green mystery. It didn't matter that she was his little sister. She was fun to be with. She was his best friend. But then she was gone, and people locked their doors, stopped speaking, stared out at the now empty street from behind closed curtains and shuttered windows. Emily was gone. The once blue sky was a perpetual bone grey. Summer was gone. Forever.

Lawrence sighed, shook the memories from his head. He tucked Emily's picture into the breast pocket of his shirt and stood. He picked up his overnight bag, and the grey coat, and walked to the exit. At the open door, he paused. Maybe the driver would come back. But he had a queer feeling that this was the bus's last stop, so he stepped out. It would be a long walk.

Clutching his bag, Lawrence headed north along the boulevard. The world was black and white, shades of grey, a chaotic chiaroscuro. Everything seemed round, slightly blurry, as if he was seeing through a lens smeared with Vaseline. Strangers walked past in long cloaks, with hunched shoulders, and hooded eyes glinting above their upturned collars. What he could see of their faces was disconcerting. They were formless, with slight depressions, like kneaded bread or clay.

He walked and walked. The soot-colored city stretched out before him. Fat black flies droned and buzzed lazily above garbage heaped on sidewalks. Dark shadows slithered silently in side alleys. Lamp posts with single, sallow eyes studied his movements. Bare, thin trees reached for him with bony fingers. The air reeked of rotted fish, spoiled milk... and blood. He could taste metal. The air thrummed and wavered. Lawrence imagined he stood in an electrical field under a great grey pylon. The wind picked up, rushed at him in a scream. Lawrence thought that underneath the wind's shriek he heard another sound. Laughter. Childhood laughter. The laughter of sweet innocence. Emily's laughter.

The overnight bag swung easily in Lawrence's hand. A soft clattering sound could be heard.

Puddles dotted the sidewalk, winking at Lawrence with an oily iridescence. On top of one puddle sat a black cowboy hat. It seemed to him that the hat's owner had simply fallen into the puddle. He remembered that scene in *The Wizard of Oz*, when the witch is doused in water and melts into the ground, leaving behind a crooked black hat. Emily loved that movie.

Lawrence remembered other movies from his youth in which the good guys wore white cowboy hats, and the bad guys wore black hats. And Lawrence knew, with dead certainty that this hat belonged to the same man who left the grey coat on the bus. He was getting close. He could feel it. It would be hard to find the disappearing man, but Lawrence knew he could. He fingered the top of Emily's Polaroid. He'd been looking for the disappearing man – looking for Emily, looking for peace—for twenty years.

The realization that the hat and the raincoat had belonged to the vanishing man both chilled and numbed Lawrence. What were the odds that *he*, of all people, could simply stumble upon these things? His stomach felt as if it were on a potter's wheel, spinning in the grip of slippery hands. He was dizzy, the muscles of his legs dissipating into the fog. Could it be? The long elusive abductor was actually near.

There had been no real indication of the vanishing man's identity. A few crazies had come forward admitting to the abduction, but their unsubstantiated claims had been dismissed by the police. There had been sightings too, but not of the man. For a brief period reports came. Sightings from Nova Scotia to Florida, following the broadcast of Emily's face on the TV news. She had been glimpsed in a shoe store in Vermont, and in the back of a pickup truck in Maine, her body alongside a dead deer. A woman supposedly spotted a wheelchair-bound Emily in a North Carolina parking garage. Then there was the elderly couple who swore they saw her legs hanging in a New Orleans butcher shop. The news had mentioned the birthmark on her left thigh—the curious splotch of pigment that resembled a human molar. While Emily sightings had poured in from all over the eastern seaboard, there never was a clear description of the man that had snatched her away.

Lawrence plucked the hat from the puddle, shoved it in the bag, and continued north through the haze. The abandoned raincoat lay folded over one arm.

He had been on this street before, but today it was different. Once there had been glossy shops and a pulse of activity, but now it was drab, the neon suffocated, and tenements loomed like monstrous assemblages of soggy cardboard. All the windows were smashed. A girl's lilting laughter floated out from one of the sad structures, a breezy chuckle that turned to a red scream.

He found himself standing on the steps outside one of the apartments. Auto-pilot had aimed him there. The sepia-colored building was vaguely familiar. As if he'd been here before. His overnight bag bounced against his leg as he ascended, making a faint clanking sound. Wind tugged at the damp coat that hung over one arm. The coat felt heavier than it had before. He unfolded it, frisked it. He had missed something the first time; it was an inside pocket opposite the one where he'd found Emily's picture. Someone had cut a slit in the lining, had sewn a discreet pouch. Lawrence reached in and felt chilly metal.

He pulled out a pistol. It was a nickel-plated snub nose .38. The revolver was small, like a sparrow in armor. It made him think of knights in childhood movies, the heroic clad in silvery suits. He thought of cowboys, too, the "good guy" with a gun at his hip, and a white Stetson.

Lawrence shoved the gun and the coat into his overnight bag. He reached for the door of the tenement, twisted the knob, and stepped inside.

A dim hallway angled off to the left, and a narrow staircase rose on his right. A high-pitched scream hit him, pinned him like a dead moth to a specimen board. He climbed the stairs, listened. Nothing. He took a step down the short, dark hallway, and stood at the first door. 2A. Then he remembered Emily, and the dream, and the two tiny words. *"To be."*

2B.

Lawrence walked to the next door, 2B, and pushed on it. It swung open, hinges squealing in protest. He stepped inside, shut the door. The apartment was completely empty. No furniture, no wall hangings, no accoutrements of any kind. A bare kitchen, cupboards forlornly open, squatted off to the left. To the right, a short hallway led to a bathroom and bedroom. Straight ahead was the living room, and a door. A tiny dirt-grimed window afforded some dim light.

He walked to the door, pulled it open, and peered into a large walk-in closet. A full-length mirror, streaked with dirt and corroded with age, covered the rear wall. He rubbed it with his free hand, polished it as best he could. Suddenly, Lawrence felt world weary. He placed his bag on the floor, sat down on the bare, warped wood, and rested.

Lawrence unzipped the overnight bag, reached in and took out the hat, the coat, the pistol, and placed them on the floor. He pulled out a cloth bundle, tied with twine. He untied the twine and spread the cloth out, revealing brittle bones like ancient twigs. Lawrence placed Emily's bones on the floor, arranged the legs in order. He trembled, squeezed his eyes shut so that the tears wouldn't leak out. Lawrence cocked his head, listened. And waited.

Shortly, he heard it – tiny, muffled screams, emanating from the closet, from beneath the wood floor. He listened until the screams petered out. Listened until he could hear, instead, Emily's innocent laughter dancing on the summer wind. And, from beneath the floor, he heard a muffled clump, as if someone were knocking.

Lawrence leaned over, inspected the cheap wood floor. He poked and pushed until a board popped up. He pried the board loose. With two hands he pulled up as many floorboards as he could. The wood was old and soft, and gave way with ease. Soon, he had a two-foot wide hole in the closet. Lawrence reached into the hole, pulled out an old, vinyl gym bag.

For a short while, Lawrence sat and stared at the gym bag. He could still hear Emily's sweet voice. In his mind, he pictured her: a smiling, blonde pixie.

He opened the gym bag, reached in and pulled out the skull. Emily's skull. He was sure of it. Then Lawrence pulled out the arms and ribcage. He assembled them on the floor, made her as whole as he could.

Lawrence stood, picked up the coat, put it on. It was a good fit. He plucked the soggy black Stetson from the floor, perched it atop his head. He glanced in the old mirror, nodded. Not bad, he thought. Next, Lawrence retrieved the pistol, turned it over in his hands. He stuck the barrel in his mouth, tasting oily metal.

He always wanted to be the good guy; the one in the white hat, riding to the rescue.

But it was too late for that.

WORSE THINGS

The cystic egg of the Artemia Salina exists in a suspended state, neither living nor dead.

❧

Dale died the day I went to the aquarium.

When I was very young I saw seahorses floating in a vast tank at the Tampa Aquarium. Seahorses, I later learned, belong to the family *Hippocampus*, derived from the Greek word *hippos*, meaning horse, and *campus*, meaning sea monster. Some of the seahorses were big. Some were small. Some green. Some brown. Still others looked like plants that waver and flutter on dark ocean floors. All the seahorses floated along with a stoic grace, slowly bobbing, as if caught in amniotic fluid, as if not yet birthed, smiling their thin, melancholic Mona Lisa smiles. Stately creatures tinged with a terrible sadness. And it was that certain sadness, that majestic melancholy, that attracted me. They reminded me of Dale. He, like me, was shy, quiet, unobtrusive. We didn't so much have a friendship, as share a quiet companionship. We knew we were the loners, the outsiders. At least, for a short time, we had each other.

But then Dale died.

He wasn't run over by a drunk driver, didn't succumb to a terrible terminal illness. No, Dale just died in his sleep, for reasons unknown. Though, truthfully, how a nine-year-old can die in his sleep is a mystery to me.

Dad told me the news. He'd received a call from Dale's mom. He stood in my bedroom doorway, shuffling awkwardly, staring past me. "Dale's dead," he said. The blood in my veins turned to ice. To this day my blood still runs cold, runs slow.

Even then—at an age when most boys are happy, carefree, running with reckless abandon through life—I was sad and lonely.

I stared long and hard at the seahorses that day, entranced by their grave beauty. It is one of the few times I recall feeling happy. Eventually, mother pulled me from the display, dragging me home. I vowed to go back, but I never did. I bet they are still there, swimming with elegance and pride, floating along on life's cruel currents.

Shortly after my visit to the aquarium the war came, and we moved to Canada. We settled in Toronto. There wasn't much money to be had. Mom worked weekends at a hair salon. Dad found part-time work at a garage, changing tires, doing oil, lube and filter jobs. Doing the menial tasks required of the lowest man on the totem pole, a draft dodger at that. And every time I heard someone say "draft dodger" on the newscasts, the voice was laced with anger and hatred. I couldn't understand why. If being a draft dodger meant not getting yourself killed, I saw no problem with that. Life, it seemed, was fleeting. Death could strike at any moment. Why hurry it along?

Toronto wasn't Tampa. Tampa was warm, the people cold. Toronto was cold, so cold, but the people warm. And downtown Toronto was a fascinatingly diverse cross-section of ethnicity: Russians, Greeks, Ethiopians, Pakistanis, Sri Lankans, and Chinese all intermingling in a heady world stew.

And it was in Chinatown, on a crisp autumn day in late September, where I saw the seahorses again.

There they were, all brown and prickly and dried out, stacked one on top of the other in a crude wooden box in the market. Dried husks. Empty shells. Inanimate. Sold as food and medicine. I wept. Seahorses are not monsters. We are. The vendor just smiled and winked at me. And I thought of Dale, imagined he was still in his bed, all dried out and prickly like a dead seahorse.

I could have made friends. I could have. But what was the point? Friends were apt to die on you.

Mom and dad, on the rare occasions I saw them, were like friendly drill sergeants, not really talking to me, but asking me questions. Was I okay? Yes. Did I need anything? No. How are you coping? Fine. Have you made any new friends? No. It got so that I would avoid them whenever possible. I'm sure they meant well. And at night, in my bedroom with the paper-thin walls, I could hear them talking about me, sometimes in whispers, sometimes in shouts. They weren't bad parents. Not really. I didn't love them. And I didn't hate them. I didn't feel a thing.

During those first few months in Toronto I met Mr. Warshawski. Mr. W., as I referred to him, lived across the hall from us. He was a friendly chap, effusive—the opposite of me—constantly coming and going at all hours. He always seemed to be out in the hallway whenever I left the apartment, as if he were waiting for me. Perhaps he was. Mr. W. liked people. And people liked him. He had small, black eyes that frightened me, though. Eyes that had seen a lot. Eyes that hid a terrible pain. I couldn't hold his gaze for long. Sometimes, as I looked through the peephole, I'd see him entering his apartment carrying a plastic bag. Something dark lay at the bottom of the bag.

I think Mr. W. saw me as a challenge, a tough nut to crack. He was always trying to win me over. I guess, in a way, he did.

"Hello, Aaron," Mr. W. would say in a faint European accent, waving a beefy hand, his eyes flashing darkly like the eyes of a crow.

I'd nod, feign a smile, and move on. He'd follow after me for a few steps, chatting amiably about anything and everything. Then, getting no response from me, he'd stop, smile, and wave. "Goodbye, Aaron. Have a good day."

On more than one occasion I noticed Mr. W. walk past the elevator and slip into the stairwell at the end of the hall. I suppose he didn't like elevators. I'd go into my apartment and stare out the window, waiting to see Mr. W. exit the building. But he never did. He never materialized. I wondered what happened to him.

So, one bright Saturday morning I stood inside our apartment, listening at the door. I heard Mr. W. exit the apartment, heard him shout a greeting to a neighbour. I waited, listened, and heard him shuffle down the hall, heard the stairwell door creak open and close. I stepped out and walked to the end of the hall. I slowly pushed open the door and stepped into the dank stairwell. It smelled of urine and sweat. I heard a faint noise from above. Gripping the handrail, I climbed the stairs. It grew darker the more I climbed. At the top of the staircase was a small landing and a door. I pulled the door wide and brilliant sunlight flooded the staircase. Blinking, shielding my eyes from the sun, I stepped through the doorway and onto the rooftop.

"Well hello, Aaron," Mr. W. called. "Good to see you. Come on over."

Mr. W. stood at the far end of the roof. His hulking presence blocked out the sun. "Come," he called, beckoning, "don't be afraid."

I crossed the pebbly surface and found myself standing in front of cages filled with pigeons. The cages were simple wooden beams with chicken wire stapled to them. The pigeons danced nervously, flapped their wings, cooed when I neared. Their eyes were small and glinted darkly, just like Mr. W's eyes.

"What do you think, Aaron?" Mr. W. asked. He was holding a pigeon in one hand, stroking it with the other.

I blinked. "Are they racing pigeons?"

Mr. W. laughed. "No. They aren't pigeons, really. They're squab."

"Squab?"

"Yes. It's like chicken, only tastier." Chicken came out sounding like chee-kin. Then Mr. W. grabbed the bird in both hands and with practiced ease twisted and bent the bird's neck. The bird lay still in his hand. He held it up. "See."

I stared at the lifeless creature. Its beady eyes glared at me. I felt nothing. My blood ran slow, slower.

He smiled, barked a laugh. "It's all right, Aaron." He placed his large hand on my shoulder, then pulled it back as if shocked. "You're so cold, boy." He shook his head. "So cold."

As if I didn't know.

186

Mr. W. produced a plastic bag and deposited the bird into it. Reaching into a cage, he grabbed two more squabs and quickly dispatched them, dropping them into the bag. His large hands moved with a deft touch. Smiling, Mr. W. snatched another bird and held it out to me. "Would you like to try it? It's easy once you get the hang of it."

I took a step back, gulped. My mouth was dry. I shook my head.

Mr. W. chuckled, placed the bird back in the cage. "Fine. No worries." The smile briefly faltered on his round face. He held up his bag of dead birds. "This is not such a difficult thing for me. There are worse things, yes? Trust me, Aaron, there are worse things."

"I better get going," I said, turning and walking back to the still open door.

I could feel Mr. W's eyes on me. "One day, then, you'll come for dinner, yes?" he said.

That night I dreamed of Mr. W. and his sausage-like fingers wringing the necks of dumb birds. I dreamed of Dale lying in his bed like a dead seahorse, all brown and dry, a husk of a thing. In the dream I stood over Dale and his eyes snapped open. And his eyes were small and cold and black like the eyes of dead birds.

ርጻይፊን

Mom and dad continued to fight. Their bickering grew louder by the day. At first, if they knew I was nearby, they tried to keep the fighting out of view. They would walk around the apartment, simmering, avoiding each other. Then, though, they didn't seem to care at all if I was present. They would harangue and threaten and provoke each other in my presence. At those times I could feel my blood thickening, slowing. And I would walk away with their angry words bouncing around in my ears.

It turns out that mom was pregnant. They didn't tell me. Why would they? I didn't, for the moment anyway, exist in their narrow world. I just noticed one day. Mom was doing the dishes and she turned to place a stack of plates in the cupboard. And I saw that she was pregnant, saw the swelling in her belly, and wondered how I could not have noticed before now. She was, to my adolescent eyes, *huge*. Mom caught me looking at her stomach. Her mouth smiled, but her eyes didn't. "It'll be okay, Aaron," she said. "Really." Then her hand fluttered up to her face like one of Mr. W's birds, and she began to cry. She fled the room, locked herself in the washroom. I sat in the cold, still kitchen, listening to the ticks in the apartment, listening to the blood hardening in my veins.

CR&D

Winter came, a harsh white world. I'd never experienced anything like it. The cold seeped into your bones and stayed there, seemingly forever, no matter how many hot chocolates you drank, no matter how long you sat huddled in front of the radiator rubbing your arms. Sometimes I'd venture out, walk around the block to watch the kids toboggan down the hill in the park. I'd stay until my face froze red, until my fingertips grew numb. Then I'd trundle home with frozen feet, back to the apartment and into my room to read comic books until I thawed out. I never really ever fully thawed out. There was always that ice-water in my veins, running slower by the day, by the second.

Mom's belly grew at an enormous rate. Each frigid day it seemed to expand outward, threatening to burst. And the winter chill deepened between my parents. The fights had almost stopped. Now there was a stony silence that seemed worse, somehow, than the stormy outbursts. They barely looked at each other. They'd given up. Eventually, my dad moved out, and Mr. Connell moved in. Mr. Connell – Roy to mom, but always Mr. Connell in my mind – was a tall, thin, severe man lacking in personality. But he had a good job. And red, red hair.

CR&D

On Saturday mornings I'd follow Mr. W up onto the roof. It was windy and cold, the snow blowing in savage swirls and eddies, taking little bites of my exposed skin. On those mornings I was a great explorer who'd ascended Everest or Kilimanjaro. And I'd

188

watch Mr. W. feed his birds and then wring their necks. On occasion, I'd also grab one of the birds and twist its neck until it lay still and dead in my hands. At those times I felt nothing. No secret glee, no secret shame or sorrow. Nothing. Later we'd drink hot chocolate from a thermos and Mr. W. would tell me war stories. There was one particular story he told me that still plays in my head like an old black and white newsreel:

"It was near the end, Aaron. We thought we'd managed to avoid them. But early one March morning they, the Germans, came scampering into town. We didn't know it at the time, but the Allied Forces were close behind them, nipping at their heels like angry dogs.

"I was about the age you are now, Aaron. Still a boy." He glanced at me, his eyes moist. *"There are times when I wish I still was a boy. I guess you could say I grew up that day, shed the skin of adolescence."*

Mr. W. wiped his eyes, coughed, and continued.

"There was me, Mama, Papa, and Kristof, my baby brother. Kristof was just a few weeks old. A tiny pink thing. He was so cute, so sweet, so innocent. We loved him, Aaron. Loved him the way you love your parents."

I could feel my blood slow to a torpid crawl. I didn't know what love was. I nodded mutely.

"We scrambled down to the root cellar. Papa had arranged it so that the door could be barred from the inside. So we huddled in the dark for what seemed hours, but were mere moments. We heard faint noises from the street, Aaron, then footsteps above us, in the house. The Germans were in the house!

"We tensed. I held my breath. Kristof, tiny Kristof, began to whimper. Even in the wan light I could see Papa's eyes grow wide. And then Kristof began to cry, to squeal. You never heard such a sound, Aaron. Never. It seemed, to me, in that small dark place, that a thousand angry crows screeched and screamed at once.

"Papa looked at me, his eyes large and bright and afraid. He nodded toward Kristof, and I tip-toed to the corner to try and placate my little baby brother. Mama sat in a corner, curled in a ball, a shawl pulled up under her chin.

"Kristof kicked, squealed, and I tried to shush him. Above us we heard the muted clatter of footsteps and cupboards slamming. I could picture the Germans stomping about the kitchen in their black boots, searching.

"It is not such an easy thing to describe, Aaron. The terror. The pure terror. My heartfelt hot and heavy, a hard lump. I grew dizzy. My vision darkened. Kristof complained. I picked him up, pressed him to my chest, tried to quiet him. He continued to cry, to fuss, so I pressed him closer to my chest, held him tighter so that he wouldn't move, couldn't move. And I held him like that as I listened to heavy black boots clumping along the floorboards. Held him tight, tighter, in that small dark place that grew still and silent, as if holding a breath. Held little Kristof tight until he himself grew still and silent, until the footsteps receded, until we were sure that it was safe, that everything would be okay and that we could come out of hiding. And I continued to hold Kristof for many days, pressed to my bosom, singing and cooing to him, until Papa pried him from my grip and buried him in the back."

When Mr. W finished his tale, he reached into one of the cages and snatched a bird from its roost. He smiled weakly and snapped its neck.

CRSO

Comic books got me through that first long, dreary winter. I got fifteen cents each week for allowance – provided my chores were done—and on Friday's after school I'd stop at Wayne's Smoke & Gift Shop to pick out a comic book: Green Arrow, Silver Surfer, Aquaman. They, and perhaps Mr. W., were my friends, my only friends. At least they wouldn't die on me.

It was in the back of a Green Arrow comic, sandwiched between ads for X-Ray Specs and Charles Atlas, where I noticed another ad, one that made me think about seahorses. Except it wasn't for seahorses, but Sea-Monkeys. There it was, page 27, red lettering on a yellow background; a smiling family watching these little alien things cavorting about, carefree.

The Wonderful World of *Amazing* Live Sea-Monkeys:

Own a Bowlful of Happiness – Instant Pets!

The picture in the ad was highly detailed. The Sea-Monkeys had big saucer eyes, and large antennae shooting from the top of their heads. And they smiled. Huge grins creased their chubby faces.

Amazing *Live* Sea-Monkeys!
Hatch a happy troupe of Sea-Monkeys!
More fun than a zoo full of chattering, howling jungle monkeys.
Only $1.25

So, for two months I saved my meager money, resisted the urge to catch up on the latest adventures of Silver Surfer. When I'd collected enough money I sent away for my bowlful of happiness. And waited. A couple of weeks later a package arrived in the mail, addressed to me. When I showed it to mom and Mr. Connell they shrugged their indifference.

In my room I opened the box. Inside was a small bowl, the type of bowl goldfish swim in. There was also some painted gravel, a couple small plastic palm trees, and a waxy white pouch. Following the enclosed instructions I filled the small bowl with warm, salty water. I cut open the pouch and poured the contents into the palm of my hand: tiny white crystals. They looked a bit like the mound of gravel that now lay at the bottom of the bowl. Were they eggs? They didn't look like eggs. I wondered idly how life could evolve from these innocuous little crystals.

I dumped about half of the tiny crystals into the water. I placed the remaining eggs in a clear plastic sandwich bag, the type that zips neatly shut, and tucked it away in my sock drawer. I waited. And waited. I sat staring at that bowl for hours, waiting for the miracle. Nothing. No stirring. No signs of life. Eventually, I finished my homework, read some old comic books, and went to bed.

The next morning dawned bright but cold. The sun slanted through my blind, spilling golden light into my room. I wanted to curl up under my bed covers and sleep and dream and do nothing. But something caught my eye and I sat up, blinking.

There was movement in the fish bowl. A ray of morning light shone on the bowl, and tiny silver sparkling specks drifted in the water, cast in a golden light.

The Sea-Monkeys had hatched!

I raced to the bowl, peered in. Sure enough, tiny creatures swam and floated and darted about in the tiny bowl. But they didn't resemble the ad in the comic book. They were tiny odd-shaped brown creatures, about half an inch long, with a small tail, not quite transparent, swimming in their little world of water. I later learned that they were actually briny shrimp, their proper name being *Artemia Salina*. For now, though, they were Sea-Monkeys. While they lacked the grace and elegance of seahorses there was something about them that moved me. Like me, they were small and vulnerable, existing in their own small world. And, for a brief moment, in my little room, with the golden morning light shining on my bowl of happiness, I felt my heart thaw.

That evening my mother gave birth to a boy. He had red, red hair and she named him Philip. Alone in my cold room, I wept.

Two weeks later all my Sea-Monkeys died.

And so did Philip.

CREO

Late in the winter, Mr. W. went missing. I hadn't seen him in a few days, and that was unusual. Mr. W. was always out and about, chatting with the neighbours. Come one Saturday I went to his door and knocked. I was eager for our trek to the rooftop.

There was no answer at his door, so I went up to the roof. It was mid-February, bitterly cold, the snow thick and heavy like a wet wool blanket. The squab cooed and clucked. They were resilient creatures, seemingly unaffected by the frigid weather. I found Mr. W. on the ground, below the cages, staring blankly up at the white sky. A thin layer of crusty ice covered him. I was reminded of the tiny white crystals, the eggs, in the drawer in my room. If I poured salty water on him, would he awake? The blood in my veins slowed to a trickle. I opened the cages to release the birds, but they stood there dumbly, cooing and clucking and bobbing their heads.

I left Mr. W. on the rooftop. At first, I shoved him under a cage. But I thought he might thaw, so I pulled him out again and left him where I found him. It wasn't likely anyone would come up here in the winter. And, that way, I'd be able to still come see Mr. W.

And I did visit Mr. W., every Saturday, like old times. The squab hadn't stayed past that first week. Their cages stood mute and empty. I'd sit in the snow beside Mr. W., cross-legged, letting the coldness soak into me. I'd stare at Mr. W., watching the snow and ice freeze over him, marveling at his stillness in his white tomb. Soon, he'd resemble the tiny hard crystals hidden away in my room. Forever frozen. It was, I thought, better to be frozen. That way you couldn't feel anything.

When the weather began to warm, when Mr. W. began to thaw, I stopped going up to the rooftop. I never went up there again. I didn't want to see what became of Mr. W.

Spring came, then summer. Nobody ever mentioned Mr. W again. Not even me. Sometimes, though, I'd sit in my room and think about him and try not to cry.

CRER

The cystic egg of the Artemia Salina exists in a suspended state, neither living nor dead.

And here I sit in my dark apartment, my blood gone cold, neither living nor dead. I hold the sandwich bag with the tiny crystals, my Sea-Monkeys, my children. I've never bothered to bring them to life. They are better this way.

A lot of time has passed, many years. Some things I've forgotten. Other memories swirl with ice-like crystalline clarity, cutting deep.

I see Dale, small, quiet, forever young. I spot the sad seahorse swimming stoically. I glimpse a troupe of Sea-Monkeys lying at the bottom of a fish bowl, still but for the faint current that buffets their tiny, dead bodies. I see Mr. W. and his round, smiling head. I witness his large hands moving with incredible deftness, snapping the necks of dumb birds. I see beady black eyes, staring. I recall standing in the small dark room, staring down at the tiny baby with the red, red hair, my hands reaching down. I remember Mr. W. saying *"This is not such a difficult thing for me."*

And, as it turns out, it wasn't such a difficult thing.

There are always worse things.

AFTERWORD:
A MURDER OF CROWS

I'm going to tell you something I did once that I'm not very proud of. Bear with me. It might seem that this has nothing to do with Michael Kelly or the book you're holding in your hands, but I'll tie it all together in the end. Trust me.

Okay, then: the deed. (Confession isn't easy, though, not when you can't see your audience, can't cue off the reaction in their eyes, can't judge the telltales of body language and so forth. This isn't a confessional, and you're no priest, so please don't draw that corollary; I'm not looking for absolution. I just need to explain the deed, but I'll have to do it at my own pace and with a bit of panache ... like I was telling a story.)

Start with this piece of information: I hate crows. They flock to my backyard, cawing and cackling, coal-black and soulless. Never one at a time; always a mercenary battalion of them. Their sentries watch from the trees or the clothesline, and if I open the back door, they flee, their clamorous, cowardly calls ricocheting between my house and the woods. If I don't go to the door and scare them away, they sit on my satellite dish. They cover it with shit that has to be scrubbed off with the hose and a Brillo pad. It's as if they're mocking me. *This is what we think of you. This is what we think of your 300 channels and your pay per view!*

The crows steal the bread and the seed that we put out for the smaller birds, even when the seed is too small for them to eat. (For that matter, do crows eat seed at all?) They arrive in force, chasing away the sparrows and cardinals and blue birds. They set up a cordon around the feeder, occupying it with niggardly military precision. Then they strut through the seed, scattering it with their umber talons, contaminating it with their midnight bouquet. They'll also steal my dog's food. They dive-bomb the squirrels, raking with their dark claws and beaks. I've seen them strut across the yard, four and five abreast, like some Nazi skirmish line, their fiendish black eyes sweeping back and forth, their heads bobbing in synch. I've watched them harass the redtail hawks that soar so stately over my property, swooping at the hawks with rapacious caws and a furious, bat-like flapping of ebony wings. They always attack en masse, never one-on-one. The hawks turn and glide swiftly away on the thermals, aristocratic to the last, but for days I'm no longer privileged with their hauntingly beautiful cries from on high.

When I chase the crows away, they circle the house, screeching like psychotic old women. Their taunts grate on my nerves and arouse in me an inexplicable hatred that's as unsettling in its intensity as it is juvenile. It's as if I'm back in elementary school and a group of bullies are circling me, calling me names, jabbing at me with sticks or tossing my book back and forth between them, just out of reach over my head; and just when I can't take their torment any longer and decide to hurl myself at every one of them, even if it means I'll take a horrible beating because they outnumber me so, they flee from me, running around the playground, laughing and chanting and teasing, denying me even the satisfaction of getting pounded senseless in exchange for the meager victory of no longer being their patsy and perhaps getting in one good lick of my own.

So I had taken to shooting at the crows. I used a 12 gauge Browning pump at first. I'd open the back door and they'd flee, but I'd run out as fast as I could, point the gun at the sky, and: *Blam! Blam! Blam!* They'd whirl this way and that, scattering but never truly reacting with the desired terror. Their calls seemed to say, "Missed us again, Hopkins! You couldn't hit one of us if we perched on the end of your gun, you loser!" And miss them I did, time and time again. It had been twenty years or more since I'd fired a shotgun at an airborne target. I sucked then, too. So I'd go out the front door and sneak around the house, trying to catch them unaware, trying to get a shot at one on the ground. Their sentries would set off the alarm, and the crows would scatter, laughing amongst themselves, throwing insults back at me. I'd go through a whole box of shells ... and the crows would circle my house, unscathed and undeterred, and oh-so-vocal about it.

I finally got out my Marlin .22 magnum bolt action—the one with the nice 3x9 Leopold scope. From a prone position, I could once put a group of shots inside a one inch circle at 100 yards with that rifle (though I'm probably out of practice now). Double the size of the grouping for a standing position, but that's still well within the kill-zone for a crow. I cracked the back door open just an inch. I sat at the kitchen table and waited, rifle in my hands, the sling wrapped around my arm for balance the way the military teaches marksmen and snipers. I'd already chambered the round. My finger was resting on the safety button. I could wait in this position for a long time. Patience is the hunter's greatest virtue.

Three or four crows flew in from the wooded valley south of my house, landed in the yard, and set up their skirmish line about fifty feet from my back door. I took aim on the lead crow, lining up the cross hairs on his chest as he strutted arrogantly through the grass. Clicked off the safety. Let out my breath. Gently squeezed the trigger.

The rifle was incredibly loud in the confines of the kitchen.

The crows burst into flight—all except one which was flopping about on the ground.

"Now!" I yelled, opening the door. "What do you think of that? Ha! I got you, you sonofabitch!"

I ran outside to revel in my victory, to stand over my conquered foe, mocking his agony, laughing at his death-throes. But--

The crow was a pitiful sight. The bullet had passed completely through his breast and then clipped his wing as it exited, shattering the bone a half inch or so from where his wing joined his body. Both ends of the broken bone were protruding. The wing hung limply, a dead thing, like a black pirate flag hanging windless from the yardarm of a sinking vessel. I don't know what I expected. I thought he would lunge at me when I got close. Strike at me with that sharp beak. Claw me with his talons. Or maybe he would run in terror, floundering helplessly on the ground in a vain attempt to take to the air and escape me. What he did, as I knelt to examine him, was lay still. Not a sound. No movement but a panting through his open beak. There was blood on his breast. Blood on his beak. Blood on the jagged edges of the brittle white bone protruding from his body and wing.

His eyes weren't impenetrably evil and dark. They were an indigo nebula of intelligence and sorrow, steady and intense and molasses soft. *What now?* He seemed to say. *Now that you've crippled me ... what now?*

I went in the house and retrieved the 12 gauge. I picked him up and carried him away from the house where my wife and my young daughter couldn't see what I had done or what I needed to do next. I was ashamed of myself. I didn't want them to know I'd finally hit one of the crows. They did know, of course, but I wanted to spare them the true knowledge of what I had done, the knowledge that only came by looking into the eyes of that poor dying animal.

The crow didn't struggle in my hands. Didn't make a sound. He just lay there, staring at me, his eyes holding that one single question: *why?* I took him into the woods. Set him down, being as careful as I could, trying not to cause him any further pain. I told him I was sorry. I asked him to forgive me. Then I ended his suffering with the shotgun.

And I never shot at the crows again.

Oh, sure, lots of people who've heard me talk about this just laugh and say, "It was just a stupid crow, Brian. I hate them, too." Or: "Hell, I've killed hundreds of crows out in the fields. Hate those damn things!" Or: "Geez, it was just an animal. Get over it." They don't see anything wrong with what I did. They wouldn't care if I shot every crow in Oklahoma.

Maybe I'm just wired different. I never again want to see something, be it a crow or a whale or—God forbid—a human being, look up at me from the threshold of death with that same question in its eyes. I never want that responsibility, that accountability, that culpability again.

Okay, then: the point to all this. What I learned that day is that the true nature of horror lies not in the extravagant monsters we invent to populate our nightmares, to frighten our children, or to entertain us at the movie theater. True horror is rooted in our own flawed humanity, in the dark deeds that we're capable of committing on a whim. True horror exists in all of us and waits only the momentary lapse in judgement, the sadistic belief in our superiority, the overpowering glee of greed, the hatred and fear and alienation resulting from race, creed, religion, culture, and our own frail fear and indifference toward the quintessential other to make its way to the surface and inspire life-altering action. True horror springs from within people no different than you and me. It's unseen and unpredictable, virulent and unforgiving and, God help us, appealing on some reptilian level.

Michael Kelly already knows this. The stories collected here prove that beyond a shadow of a doubt. Let me say it again: Michael Kelly understands the true nature of evil. He's comfortable with it. He doesn't mind getting intimate with it. He refuses to shirk the responsibility that every good storyteller has for documenting the true depths of the human heart in all its gory glory. For this reason, Michael Kelly knows how to frighten us.

This is uncommon. For every writer who grasps this relatively obvious secret, there are a hundred others slinging meaningless buckets of blood against their computer screen hoping some of it will stick, a hundred others whose inexplicable monsters crawl out of the bog and chow down on their throw-away characters, a hundred others whose novels are brimming with pointless zombies and vampires and ... you get the picture. Michael Kelly knows the real monster lives across the street from you.

More to his credit, Michael also understands the duality of evil, that no force in the universe is without its opposite. To make his stories work, to make them connect with every reader who must believe in more than the evil that lurks within, Michael Kelly populates his fictional universe with hope and redemption, self-sacrifice and devotion, compassion and commitment and love. It's when these human constructs stand against the dark forces that true, memorable storytelling is accomplished. It's then that life is mirrored in fiction so that we can study who and what we are, learn what we're made of, and walk away with a better understanding of our place in the universe.

Brian A. Hopkins
at Road's End, Oklahoma City
January 17, 2007

PUBLICATION HISTORY

Scratching the Surface originally appeared in *Dark Arts*, ed. John Pelan, Cemetery Dance, 2006.

Thin Red Wire originally appeared in *Scratching the Surface*, 2007.

Comes a Cool Rain originally appeared in *Northern Horror*, ed. Edo van Belkom, Quarry Press, 1999.

Like a Stone in the Riverbed originally appeared in *Fusing Horizons*, 2004.

Radiant Boxer originally appeared in *Scratching the Surface*, 2007.

The Simple Sound of Dead Trees Singing originally appeared in *All Hallows*, 2006.

A Place of Stones and Thorns originally appeared in *Scratching the Surface*, 2007.

Warm Wet Circles originally appeared in *Alone on the Dark Side*, ed. John Pelan, RoC, 2006.

Paper Thin originally appeared in *The Dark Krypt*, 2006.

Metastasis originally appeared in *Plum Ruby Review*, 2004.

Summer Ghosts originally appeared in Scratching the Surface, 2007.

Sea of Ash and Sorrow originally appeared in *Reflection's Edge*, 2007.

The Man Who Ate Moths originally appeared in *Feral Fiction*, 2005.

Twilight in the Field of Forever originally appeared in *Flesh & Blood #13*, 2003.

Last Train Home originally appeared in *Deadbolt #2*, 1998.

When Children Weep originally appeared in *The Book of Dark Wisdom #6*, 2005.

The Smell of Chaos is Written in its Hues originally appeared in *Scratching the Surface*, 2007.

Wolves & Angels originally appeared in *Scratching the Surface*, 2007.

Boulevard of Broken Dreams originally appeared in *Scratching the Surface*, 2007.

Worse Things originally appeared in *Scratching the Surface*, 2007.

UNDERTOW

PUBLICATIONS

2013

www.ingramcontent.com/pod-product-compliance
Lightning Source LLC
Chambersburg PA
CBHW050841180626
46814CB00007B/2574